BROKEN SILENCE

Author By:

Carolyn M. Taylor

Table Of Content

CHAPTER 1

The Last Fight

Jean, my sister, called me crying. She said Dad had jumped on Mama and choked her.

My entire body filled with anger. It took everything in me not to go over there immediately, but I needed to be smart. I told Jean not to worry; I would take care of it.

She said, “Please don’t do anything stupid.”

“I won’t do anything stupid,” I said. “I’ll make it classy… how about that?”

“Classy?” she yelled. “What does that even mean?”

“Girl, just trust me,” I added.

I paced the floor all night. Didn’t get a wink of sleep—just waiting on daybreak.

It was the longest night ever… but morning finally came.

I made sure Mama had left for work and my sisters had gone to school. The coast was clear.

I put on my favorite red high-heeled shoes—six inches high, may I add—because I was determined to make a statement that day. It was the perfect day, too. The man didn't work on Mondays.

I rang that doorbell and beat on the door like I was trying to break it in.

He opened it quickly and looked surprised to see me. Then came that same old mean face—the one I'd known all my life.

"Get the hell off my property, bitch," he said.

At that point, words like that didn't bother me. I wasn't there for that anyway. I was there for one reason and one reason only, my mother.

Without wasting time, I calmly stuck my hand out and pointed down to my shoes.

Yes—my red pumps. Six inches high.

The man looked down.

That's when I drove into his chest as hard as I could, sending him stumbling backward through the house like he'd lost his balance completely.

I wanted this day to go down in history—to never be forgotten by him.

"So you put your hands on my mama again, didn't you?" I said. "Let's make sure that won't happen again."

He was still trying to get up.

"You know my mama, right? The kind and lovely woman you've been choking and bullying for years… yeah, her. Well, this is for her."

The man made it halfway up, and I knocked him back down. I saw Mama's face in my head, and something in me switched on.

I punched him repeatedly. He didn't have a chance to throw a single punch. The blood from his mouth and head didn't slow me down at all. All I could see was my mama's face.

When I finished, I stood over him and pressed my red pumps against his thick neck until he struggled to breathe.

Then I said, "Next time, think before you speak."

Those were the exact words he had said to me after he nearly killed me when I was about nine years old.

I walked out with a twist in my hips and a swing in my arms, leaving the door wide open so he would get the full picture. I didn't care if he reported me or not.

Yet no police ever came looking for me. I suppose the man was too embarrassed to admit it was his own child who beat him. He never told Mama that story, and neither did I.

Mom and I talked a lot on the phone. She told me that some guys had jumped Randy and hurt him badly.

I said, “Oh wow… I wonder why.”

I told her to tell him to be careful because people like that could come back.

She said, “I will be sure to tell him what you said.

CHAPTER 2

It's a Boy!

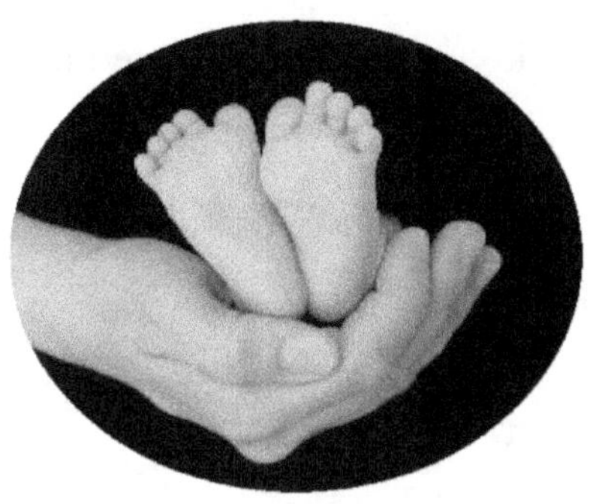

Did you hear about the excitement coming from Room 333? They say I was the center of attention. And according to the rumor, you would've thought the Falcons had won the Super Bowl, that's what they say.

Just shy of a year before my birth, my mom brought forth four girls all in one day. That delivery should've been something to talk about. Even triplets would have been a shocker, but quadruplets were practically unheard of.

My sisters were born August 5th, and I was born the following year, June 30th. Yep, that was pretty darn close, don't you think? I'm sure they made a mistake. But "they say" it was the most exciting day of all. Why? I'll tell you why. Because the man wanted a boy just that bad. So, there you have it out I jumped with a ding-a-ling, and the crowd shouted… "It's a boy!" The man was the happiest man in town, according to Uncle Joe.

Uncle Joe would definitely make some kid an excellent father. I'm just glad to be his nephew.

Jack B. Quick was the talk of the town. Yes, that's me. Our last name was Quick, and my folks named me Jack. And they had the nerve to put the "B" in the middle, but it stood for nothing, just like Jack, absolutely nothing. Normally, Christian people named their children after themselves or someone in the Bible. The man named me all by himself, Mama said, like that was something brilliant.

I know Mama would have come up with something a little better than the name Jack. It's such a masculine name. And it doesn't fit me.

Uncle Joe mentioned in his sermon that names don't make a person; people make their names. I thought that was pretty cool. So, Jack it was… for then.

Then I realized I couldn't be who I am until I was out of the man's house. Because in the man's house, he set the rules and he called the shots. If I managed to live through his house and make it to adulthood, that would be a surprise. So, surprise—I made it. But the way things were looking back then, one of us was likely to kill me. That's just the way I felt.

The man had a few good things he'd do. Nothing to write home about. He was an outstanding handyman. Mama could have hired a handyman if that's why she married him. But yeah, he was always working around the house, fixing things and making things. You would think he had ADD… I learned about that in the third grade. It's not just children who have it—adults can have ADD too.

The man loved barbecuing and cleaning the yard. He would cut the neighbors' grass too sometimes. He didn't even charge folks. That was nice. Those are good things I can say about the man. I'm still searching my brain for at least three good things about him to add to all the rotten stuff. I would hope there is some good in everyone.

Our neighbors would come home and find their grass nicely cut. You see, things like that the man was good at. Oh yeah, fishing. Fishing was his number one thing to do. Though fishing itself isn't considered a "good thing," the fact that he shared his catch with the neighbors was. So there you have it… the good of the man, all in a nutshell.

Okay, back to my birth. I reckoned I was pretty cool; after all, I came into this world all by myself. They say the man was skipping around the hospital, passing out peppermint sticks instead of cigars. Uncle Joe said he lost fifty dollars to the man in that boy/girl bet. “Your old man was pretty confident that time,” said Uncle Joe.

Uncle Joe said that my dad didn’t want any more children after my arrival because now he was totally satisfied. A man is incomplete until he brings a boy into this world, thus said the man.

But here’s the funny thing. The man didn’t really win the bet at all. He owes Uncle Joe that little fifty dollars back. I am a girl, and the man doesn’t even know it. If bringing a boy into this world makes a man complete, then he is in bad shape.

The man’s real name is Rusty, but he hated that name, according to Uncle Joe. He pretty much changed his name himself to Randy. Rusty—what’s wrong with Rusty? It sounds much better than some nursery rhyme—Jack. Jack be nimble, Jack be quick, Jack jumped over the candlestick… blah, blah, blah.

CHAPTER 3

Walking On Eggshells

My folks and I went to church every time the doors opened. The man was addressed as Deacon Quick, and Mama was Sister Quick. The five of us sat on the same pew with Mama every service. The deacons had their special corner, and the little old ladies had theirs.

I knew to sit still and follow the church routine. I didn't like church, and I hated dressing up every Sunday like a boy. Plus, it was boring, and it didn't make sense. A talking snake, human sacrifice, killing animals to please a god, eternal suffering as a form of punishment—the list goes on. I wasn't supposed to ask questions, either.

As I got older, I remember wanting to ask two simple questions in Sunday school. I managed to ask one of the two before I was shot down. Actually, I should have never opened my mouth. I saw the man leave with the offering pan, so it was my perfect opportunity. By the way, to my surprise, the man was sitting in the back. But nonetheless, my first question was, what is the evidence of the Christian God?

Someone in the back blurted out, "What do you mean the Christian God, as if there is another God? The Christian God is the one and only God."

Then I said, "I'm sorry, I thought there were more, since the Bible says to worship no other gods before me. But nevertheless, let's forget I said that. Please answer the initial question—what is the evidence of God?"

One smart guy said, "Look outside and see the trees. Where do you think they come from?"

"I don't know," I replied, "but if you know, then please state your evidence and not your opinion. I'm simply asking for evidence of God. What you gave me was your opinion on how trees got here. If you don't have evidence for the question, then just say… I don't have evidence. It's okay."

Then one of the deacons yelled, "We don't have to have evidence because we have faith." Everybody clapped as if he had won a Nobel Prize.

But I thought that was the stupidest thing to say. It didn't make a bit of sense. Everybody knows faith is just believing something without evidence.

Stating that God created the trees, the moon, and the sun is no less or more than me saying Bigfoot did it. No evidence for either. Trees are only evidence that they exist, not evidence that a god created them.

I told myself to just shut up, because I was already in trouble with the man.

I wasn't saying that there wasn't a god. I wasn't implying that fully. I was just asking for evidence. I truly wanted to believe—just give me the damn evidence so I could.

These church folks get so offended about their doctrine—something they seem to know very little about. They don't even realize that there are hundreds of gods, and every group believes their god created the trees and everything else. How do I know which god is the one, if any? That's all I'm saying.

I have questions about my daddy, whom I see every day, so surely I've got questions about a god that I've never seen. Yes, I have a truckload of questions.

The man would occasionally look over at me during service for whatever reason—probably wishing he could have dropped me off at the nearest gas station.

He chewed me out when we got in the car for asking stupid questions. Mama didn't say a word, as usual.

It was within that year we left that church and joined Uncle Joe's church. It wouldn't surprise me the least if they left because of me. I was probably ruining the man's reputation.

We still sat on the same row together with Mama. The man was still called Deacon Quick, and Mama was still called Sister Quick.

It really wasn't my uncle's church; he was just hired to preach there. My uncle was more of a motivational preacher, which was a million times better. Sometimes he didn't even open the Bible or recite a single scripture. I'm almost sure my folks never noticed that.

Nearly every Sunday, on the way home, the man would say, "Jack, you embarrassed me again."

We all knew what he was talking about.

That's why I didn't like going. I always had to walk on eggshells. Mama didn't say a word; I guess she only talked when they were alone. And, too, the Bible states that the woman is to be submissive to her husband—another question I needed an answer to.

The man made an important announcement when we got in the car. He said, "From now on, Jack, don't move out of your seat at church. When offering time comes around, you are to remain seated. Don't even stand to clap your hands. We will continue this routine until I feel that you know how to walk like you are supposed to. The only time you are to walk is when service is over. Understand?"

"Yes, sir," I replied.

"And by the way, that nonsense you did at the other church will not be brought to this one."

Bingo. So I was the reason for their leaving. This was actually the third church my folks had joined that year.

The only way I'm going to live through this is to get sick and have my folks carry me around in a wheelchair. Other than that, I'm going to stay in trouble. I can't do anything right. Even just breathing is a problem with the man.

Mama stopped giving me a dollar to carry to the offering table.

"By the way, Jack," the man asked, "did you pay attention to the ceremony today?"

"A little," I said.

"Where was your mind at, Jack? I was ordained to be the head deacon today, and that's something to be proud of."

Jean interrupted, "What's the difference, Dad?"

"Oh, baby," the man gladly answered, "it's about as much difference as being a student versus being the teacher. Big difference, right?"

"Yes, sir," Jean said. "Huge difference. So, do you tell the other deacons what to do?"

"Pretty much like that," the man responded.

"Wow, can a lady be a deacon, too?" Jean asked.

"No, dear. But maybe Jack would like to be a deacon one day. Would you care to be a deacon when you grow up, Jack?" the man asked.

Inside my head, I yelled, "Hell no!" But my mouth said, "Yes, sir."

"Well," the man responded, "you need to man up and act like it."

CHAPTER 4

About Them Church Folks

Mama and I could talk for hours when the man wasn't around. But she had little to nothing to say about him. I'd say a little something, but I kept it short and simple.

The man kept his disciplinary tools sharpened for me, so I tried to stay out of his way. Mama continued being that submissive wife, keeping quiet about her true thoughts. I suppose she'd ask questions when they got home from church, like the Good Book says.

There was nothing I could do to stay out of trouble when it came to church. The man would always find fault, one way or another. Mama and I got a kick out of talking about those church folks when it was just the two of us.

We talked about Ms. Blade and how she was in line for a miracle; Deacon Bubble, the deacon who nearly hated the man; the preacher, and how his spit would fly across the room while preaching. We talked about the mischievous children running around the pulpit like it was a playground. We would laugh about the usher who would approach adults during service and hold her hand out to take their gum.

Oh, and let's not forget Mrs. Jones—she would lose her wig during the praise service every time. Last but not least was

Mrs. Jackson. That lady literally danced right out of her panties one Sunday. She only had one leg in; the panties were hanging around her ankle. She was scooting all over the place while her panties got hung from one chair leg to another. It was quite obvious the ushers didn't want to touch them. I sat there and watched the entire episode and I got in big trouble with the man for laughing.

I'm sure he was just sitting there looking at me while I was glued in on Mrs. Jackson's panties.

Speaking of Ms. Blade, she was really excited about her doctor's appointment coming up in three weeks. She gave her testimony about how excited she was. Ms. Blade was blind, but the surgeon told her she would get her eyesight back. She'd been blind for almost a year, but this particular doctor was known for his excellent work.

I asked Mama, "Who gets the credit when Ms. Blade gets her eyesight back—God or the doctor?"

She said, "God would get the credit because He's guiding the doctor's hand. And the doctor is nothing without God." Mama was being sarcastic, I think, and only repeating what she'd heard the preacher say.

I was still a kid, but she valued my boldness—thinking outside the box.

"Why does Ms. Blade need the doctor if God is going to do the healing?" I asked Mama. "Why can't God just do it without the help of a doctor, since He's going to get the credit anyway?"

Mama thought for a moment… and then another… and then another. Finally, she looked at me and said, "That's a good question, but I don't have the answer."

Then I asked another question. "What if she doesn't receive her sight after the surgery—then who is responsible for that?"

"Well," Mama said, "I don't know that either, but I've been told that God always has the final say-so."

"Really? Does the Bible say that?"

"Well, that may have come from the preacher," she laughed.

"Mom, why should we believe the Bible?"

"Because," she responded.

"Because what?"

"Because it's the Word of God!" she exclaimed.

"And how do you know that?" I asked.

"I don't know that for sure, but all my life, I've been told that the Bible was the Word of God. So I accepted it to be true."

"But what if it's not?"

"But what if it is?" she responded.

Last question, Mama. "Did you do any research on Dad before you married him?"

"Very little to none, my child," and we both laughed.

"Well, it looks like you've done the same thing with the Bible."

"How about that," Mama agreed.

Mama didn't mind me playing around and asking questions about God, the Bible, the church, or anything. But I chose not to bring up my personal issues with her because I knew she wasn't ready for that.

Mama would never say, "That's enough," or change the subject. The big day came, Ms. Blade had the surgery. Hallelujah! The surgery went well, but not as well as she expected. Ms. Blade received 40 percent of her eyesight. That was still great because she couldn't see at all before the surgery.

And there went my question. "Mom, does God get the credit for the forty percent or the doctor? I'm sure if God had anything to do with it, it would have been a hundred percent, right? So, hooray for the doctor! Right, Mom?"

"Well," Mama said, "I don't know the answer to that either, but let us be happy for Ms. Blade for now."

Mr. James stood up one Sunday and gave his testimony in church, but it didn't make a bit of sense. I understood what he was saying, but it still didn't make any sense. The poor man was in tears trying to tell the story. He informed the church that the tears were tears of joy.

Mr. James was diagnosed with an illness that was going to cost him an arm and a leg in medication every month, up in the thousands, he said. He didn't know what he was going to do. But hallelujah and glory to God, he shouted. The tears started flowing when he announced how God fixed it for him.

According to Mr. James, he received a phone call informing him that he was approved for a particular program that was going to pay for his medication in full each month. He said even the receptionist said, "Look at God, isn't He good." You see, Mr. James wasn't going to have to pay a dime! Wow, what a blessing!

Ain't God good!

All the time,

And all the time… hmm.

God is good.

I asked Mama what was crazy about that testimony, in her opinion. And all she said was, "I know, Jack. I know what you're thinking… I'm thinking too."

Hooray for Mama—for thinking!

I said, "Mom, why would an all-powerful God make sure Mr. James, or anyone, is approved for medication? Drugs. Is He or is He not capable of healing—eliminating medication? If He has the power to pay bills, can't He use that same power to heal?

Shouldn't folks' common sense kick in right about there? Why can't people see that this stuff is nothing but baloney? It's like they don't know to think, or they've been hypnotized not to. Medicine has side effects, and I know that. But if there is an all-knowing God, then He'd know it too, right?"

I was just getting started, but the man walked in, and our conversation ceased. He gave me that angry look again. I wondered if Mama had ever noticed him sharing that face with me.

He didn't speak to me, which was normal. Instead, he started talking to Mama as if they had been talking all along. I quickly found my way out, but not before giving him the middle finger, which was tucked in my pocket.

CHAPTER 5

Ear Hustling Gone Wrong

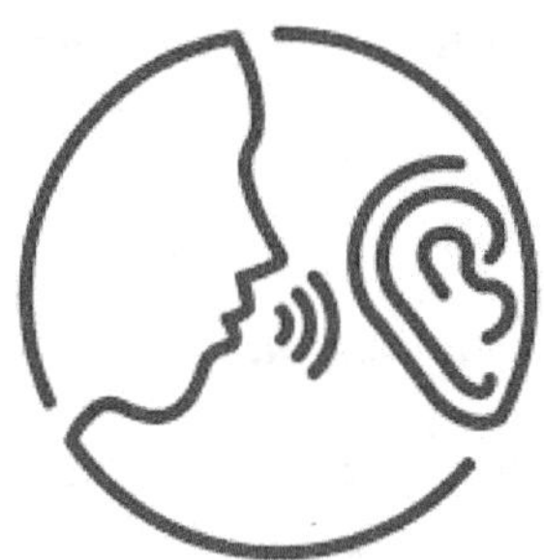

I remember this day like it was yesterday. I wasn't even a preteen at the time; I had to be eight or nine years old. This was when the ball started rolling out of control. Yeah—when the man first started growing his dislike for me.

"Shirley, is Jack getting worse to you?"

"Worse, like what?" Mama asked.

"Just worse, honey—you know what I mean."

"But worse like what?" she asked again.

"Shirley, it's not a complicated question. A simple yes or no answer would be sufficient."

"Okay, then no—he's not getting worse."

A few days later, the conversation came up again.

"Shirley, does Jack favor the girls a lot?"

"Well, yes, I suppose so—they are siblings."

"Yeah, but does he look that much like them?"

"I guess you could say so, honey. What's the problem?"

"The problem is, I can't take the boy fishing without somebody calling him a girl."

"They do the same thing with me, dear, but I know he's a boy, so it doesn't bother me that much."

"Well, it bothers me that much. Even going to the farmer's market, I'll be damned if they aren't saying the same thing down there. He won't be going there anymore. I guess the overalls don't mean a darn thing. And the fact that I'm calling him 'boy' doesn't mean a freaking thing either. What father calls his son 'boy' if he's not a boy? It's just crazy, and I'm fed up with it!"

The man was really saying he wanted nothing more to do with me. He said he was fed up with it meaning he was fed up with me.

And he meant it more than Mama could ever imagine. I know because he had already gotten rid of me for the most part. Mama just didn't know it. He only had a few more drops of hope left to change me, but even that was wearing thin.

That's what I get for ear hustling.

Mama waited patiently for the man to stop talking before she added, "He looks like you, dear."

"No, he doesn't!" the man quickly replied in his strong voice. "He looks like the girls, just like them."

"Well, the girls favor you," Mama said slowly.

Sometimes Mama doesn't know when to be quiet.

"No, they don't!" the man raised his voice more, as if it was Mama's fault. "They don't look like me at all. They all look like each other. They don't even look like you, you said so yourself."

Finally, Mama hushed.

There was a long breath of silence until Mama opened her mouth again.

" Maybe we should take this to the church. I mean, maybe someone else has experienced the same thing, and maybe—"

"No!" the man interrupted. "I don't want those undeveloped church folks talking crazy stuff about me."

"About you?" Mama questioned.

"Yes. The tree always falls on me. And I'm sure those nuts at the church would love to know that I'm having family issues."

"Randy, why do you think like that?"

"Because I feel like that, Shirley."

"But listen, honey," Mama spoke softly, "I wasn't talking about having a meeting with the congregation. I was talking about discussing it with the pastor and the board that's it."

"That's it? The pastor and the blame board? Woman, are you crazy? What do we look like telling our business to them? They have their own problems. You see, Shirley, you're too darn trusting. There you go, all willing and ready to trust them, those stupid hillbillies, with our business. Now, how dumb is that? Do they have problems?"

"Of course they do. But do they bring their problems to us? No, they don't! I'm totally surprised at you, a woman of such intelligence, to think those buffoons have answers. They are just as empty-headed as they come."

"Randy, you shouldn't call church people stupid or buffoons. They are our brothers in the Lord."

"I call it like I see it, Shirley. And let the truth be told, they are not my brothers in anything. Jesus said his family is those who do the will of his Father. Those buffoons are only doing the will of themselves. So again, there is nothing they can do for me."

"Okay, okay," Mama repeated. "The board doesn't have to be included. It can be the pastor and the two of us—how about that?"

"No way!" the man shouted. "Not Pastor Joe either. I'm already wondering what he keeps talking to Jack about so quietly—better not be talking about me. He knows too much about my business anyway."

“I suppose so, Randy, since y’all grew up as neighbors. He can’t help but know something about you. You know things about him, I’m sure.”

“No, I don’t. I don’t know one blamed thing about your brother. But you’re right, Shirley, I should know something about him. But I don’t. Not a thing. I can’t even think of one girlfriend he may have had.”

“None of that stuff is important anyway, Randy.”

“Really, Shirley? It was pretty darn important when you brought the subject up. But now that I’ve got questions about Pastor Joe, your brother—all of a sudden, it’s not important.”

“No, that’s not it,” Mama exclaimed. “Here’s the thing. Joe has never been the type who liked attention. He wasn’t into all the gossip and drama when he was coming up. He stayed to himself and was just a laid-back kind of guy. That’s probably why you don’t know much about him.”

“Really, Shirley, exactly how laid-back was the dude—was he blamed dead?”

“No, of course he wasn’t dead,” Mama added.

“Okay, if he wasn’t dead, then I should know something about him.”

“I’m just saying, honey, don’t worry about the past and what you don’t know about Joe—that’s irrelevant.”

"Irrelevant my butt! I want to know why in the heck I don't know a darn thing about your brother, since we grew up as next-door neighbors. But again, it sounds like you're taking up for him, as always. And you're trying to use reverse psychology on me, so stop."

"Okay, Randy, enough already. What about Jack, your son, what about him?"

Silence was back in the room again until the man broke the ice.

"Are there any gays in your family, Shirley?"

"Nope, not at all," Mama responded with confidence.

"You mean 'nope' as in… not that you know of."

"No, Randy, I mean nope as in nope."

"Yeah, but nobody can be a hundred percent sure of their family's personal lives," the man said.

"Now, Randy, maybe you aren't a hundred percent sure about your family, but I'm totally sure about mine. Remember, it's only two of us—Joe and me. Joe is our pastor, and you and I both know he's not gay."

"I would hope not," the man interrupted, "because the hell if I'm gonna be a part of a gay man's church."

"Right, right, right," Mama continued, trying to move things along. "You know, Randy, my mom and dad were happily married for over forty years. And they got along quite well. They were always together. They loved each other—I promise."

"Yeah," the man said. "Okay, cool."

It got quiet again until Mama asked the man the same question.

"So, what about you, Randy? Do you have any gays in your family?"

"Not that I know of, Shirley, and I'm getting quite tired now. My mind needs resting. So let's just call it a night. Goodnight, Shirley."

Sounds to me like the man got a tad bit offended or felt rather uncomfortable when Mama asked him the same question. When he said, "Goodnight, Shirley," it really meant, shut up, Shirley.

Then I made a wrong move, and the stupid shelf broke loose, causing me to tumble down from my hiding place. I was exceedingly embarrassed, lying there at the man's feet.

They both stared at me in surprise. The man put me on a thirty-day punishment and gave me that look—as if he could drive his fist through my head and have no mercy. I promise you, the stare was much worse than the punishment. But yeah, thirty blame days… just for a little ear hustling.

After all, I did hurt my elbow, my knee, and my big toe—but did anybody ask me if I was okay? No. When the man grounds you, he sticks to it with no mercy. Mama would have let me off and just given me her final words. You know the kind: "You better not ever do that again, and I mean it!"

But nonetheless, that ended my ear-hustling days.

CHAPTER 6

At The Barber Shop

"Let's go, boy," the man said rudely. I knew to stop everything, ask no questions, and obey his command. I couldn't believe he was telling me to come tag along with him.

I wasn't doing much of anything—just my homework—but that wasn't important. My education had never been his concern. I guess that was Mama's job.

The man didn't say a mumbling word while we were riding. He could have at least mentioned where we were going. That would have been a nice way to strike up a conversation. I considered asking a question or two, but his facial expression quickly put an end to that thought.

After all, it wasn't a normal thing for me to jump in the car with him anymore.

We ended up at the barber shop. I guessed the man was going to get his hair cut, because I had just gotten mine cut two days ago. He was told to wait just a few minutes—which, I'm sure, felt like the longest few minutes to him.

A lady started complimenting me out loud. "Wow," she said, "a lady would kill for those bright eyes and long lashes. Even your eyebrows are perfect."

Tapping her friend on the knee, she added, "Look at that beautiful face."

The man turned around and said, "He—is—a boy!"

But the ladies paid him no attention. It was as if they didn't like him already.

Her friend wasted no time putting her two cents in. "Oh my, you are a beautiful kid with such outstanding eyes."

I gave a smile as my thank you. I didn't dare say anything.

I knew she had a lot more to say because she was making a pretty loud statement just sitting there saying nothing. Her nails were as long as her fingers, her eyelashes were way too much, and

I could have easily jumped through her earrings. Oh, and let's not forget her lips, they were painted ashy silver. And the whole time she was talking, she was pointing her long finger this way and that way, doing the neck thing while tooting her silver lips upward. Could you imagine that?

I'm not mad at her, though. It was a sign of confidence and boldness, even if it was wild and a little creepy. She wasn't hurting anyone. She may have scared a few, though.

"Honey," she continued, slowly using one word at a time, "people are paying good money to rock lashes like yours. But yours are real, what a privilege."

The man was acting like he was so into his phone, but I knew that was a front. He didn't care to hear nice things said about me. I could feel his blood boiling. I didn't know whether I should say thank you or what, so again, I just smiled. I, too, loved my eyes and lashes, and I loved getting the compliments.

I still didn't understand why I was told to tag along, since I didn't need a haircut. It wasn't like he wanted to talk with me. My first thought was maybe he was trying to impress Mama—leading her to believe that he and I were bonding. Well, long story short, that wasn't true at all.

Finally, someone beckoned for the man to come to the back. I'm sure he was glad. He would've rather eaten mess and chased rabbits than sit there listening to those ladies.

I thought I would remain in the waiting room until he was done, but he signaled for me to follow him. He motioned with his head for me to get in the chair. What! There I went like a sheep to the slaughter, thinking, "What on earth am I getting in this chair for?"

I've been getting in this same barber chair for years, but this day was different. When I first started coming here, I needed assistance just to climb up into it.

Mr. Steve is the owner of the shop. He would make some kid an awesome father.

It never failed—he would always share a story about something he thought was amazing. And before I realized it, the haircut would be over.

He'd start off by saying, "Have you heard about the amazing things a giraffe can do?"

Every time, I'd respond, "I'm not sure."

Then he'd hand me a picture of a giraffe, or he'd say, "Have you heard about the amazing way sheep live?"

And as always, I'd say, "I'm not sure." He would hand me a picture of sheep. I'd sit there staring at it while Mr. Steve told the story. I promise you, he's probably told me over a hundred amazing stories since I started sitting in that chair.

Not long ago, he told me about how amazing kangaroos are. It's funny how he always used the word amazing, but I understood, it fit every story. Many times, I'd rush home just to look things up and learn more. And sure enough, he was right every time.

Mr. Steve is an excellent barber, and he would make an excellent teacher and an excellent dad. It may sound crazy, but he would have been a wonderful husband for my mother. She would have been happy with him.

Like I said, the man didn't say a word—he just motioned everything with his eyes and head. I doubt Mr. Steve has ever cared much for him. I'm almost sure he only deals with him for business's sake. After all, who likes people with stinking attitudes?

The man handed Mr. Steve a picture of God knows what. You wouldn't believe what happened to me that day. He had Mr. Steve skin my head. Yes—shave it down to a shiny scalp.

At first, Mr. Steve looked at the picture, then at the man, and whispered, "Are you sure?"

With all the attitude in the world, the man said, "Yes, I am." I could see them both in the mirror.

Mr. Steve tapped me on the shoulder and asked, "Do you want"

But the man cut him off, "It doesn't matter what he wants."

That was humiliating. I could tell Mr. Steve felt awkward, too.

I guess the picture was an onion, because that's exactly what I looked like when he finished. Tears immediately started rolling. I stared at myself in the mirror and saw the ridiculousness: some hair stuck to my tears, my scalp itched, but I refused to scratch.

Of all my years in that chair, Mr. Steve had never failed to share one of his amazing stories. But this time was different, he didn't utter a single word about anything amazing.

Had the man lost his everlasting mind?

And, to put the icing on the cake, I had to walk past the ladies who had once admired me, couldn't take their eyes off me, thought I was beautiful, and made me feel good inside. Now, all their pleasant thoughts about me were destroyed. The man had shown them.

There was nothing cute about my eyes or lashes anymore. All that cutie-cute stuff went out the window. Now, the attention was on my stupid, shiny bald head.

The ladies didn't say goodbye or anything as I crept by. I assumed they were in shock. They couldn't miss the tears running down my face and the fact that I had turned into an alien. I could feel all eyes on me, but I dared to raise my head.

I continued walking, looking down at the floor toward the man's feet. He walked much slower this time. No doubt he was showing off his artwork. I wanted nothing more than to feel the air hit my face, signaling freedom.

The man took his time opening the door. I was just waiting, ready to escape. Finally, I felt the air, and I was out—but the party had just begun. If only I could disappear.

The lady with the bigger mouth had something more to say. She opened the door behind us, and this is what she shouted:

"You low-down, dirty man! Ignorant you are! You can't change that child's inside by cutting her hair like that. You can't change her any more than you can change the race you were born with. It is what it is, and that's that! You may have won many battles in your life, Mr. Stupid, but you can't win this one. It's already done!"

Then she turned to me. "Baby girl, don't you feel embarrassed. You are still beautiful. Your beauty comes from the inside, and that's why it shines on the outside. You are beautiful with or without hair, and don't you ever forget that. But your dad stinks! He is funky on the outside because he's rotten on the inside!"

Wow. What a word. She should be a preacher. Honestly, she had more fire and boldness than any preacher I'd ever seen. I would actually look forward to going to church if she were the one speaking.

It made me feel a little better to know they still thought I was pretty. And the fact that she still insisted I was a girl—well, that only seemed to make the man more furious. So, he hadn't won the battle after all.

I wanted to turn around and look at her, but I knew if I did, I'd probably turn into a pillar of salt. I could see that the man was uncomfortable and livid at the same time. He kept walking as if he hadn't heard a word, though he heard every syllable loud and clear, everybody did.

He even had to stop for traffic, giving the lady even more time to preach like she was downtown on Sunday morning. When I finally opened my door, I stole a quick peek back. There she was, standing on the edge of the sidewalk, commanding attention like a true fire-and-brimstone preacher.

I sniffed, trying to cry quietly, but the man could hear me, no doubt. He didn't bother asking if I was okay.

Finally, I cried out loud, "I don't like this haircut."

The man didn't speak. He just pulled the car over recklessly and yelled, "Get out!"

Not knowing what he was about to do, I obeyed his command. I knew he couldn't grow my hair back, so I braced myself.

What was he going to do?

Was he going to run me over?

It felt like the only thing left for him to do.

As I stepped out, he directed me to press my back against the car. From his pocket, he pulled out a fingernail clipper.

If he was going to kill me, I thought, please do it quickly. Don't make me suffer.

Who in their right mind would do something like this to their child—or any child?

"Close your eyes and don't move!" he ordered.

One hand pressed my forehead back, and with the other, he clipped my eyelashes down to nothing.

I cried out loud this time. Tears poured freely, and I couldn't stop, even if he told me to. I wept, my eyes raw and scratchy.It was clear he hated the day I was born. I hated it too.

He meant to hurt me, to get back at those ladies. And in that moment, he had won. Yep. He won.

He couldn't have cared less that I had to go to school looking like Bozo the Clown—red, tired, stupid-looking eyes, and don't forget the alien head. None of it mattered to him, because to him, I stunk to his nostrils.

CHAPTER 7

Left To Die

Mama finally made it home from work and saw me standing there. She froze in her steps and stared at me with her mouth wide open. I stood there with tears rolling down my face, and I was not playing either.

Those were real tears, because I had been ripped apart inside. Mama grabbed me and held me in her arms, and I cried like a baby. I was so glad to be in her arms—someone who loved me. She whispered, “It doesn’t look that bad, and besides, it will grow back before you know it.”

You know, some perfectly shaped head kid could probably pull off the bald look, I suppose—but my head wasn’t made to be bald. My head looked funny, especially in the back. I could feel how flat it was back there.

Does he even care how many times I wished I was dead?

Would he even care that the thought of killing myself has crossed my mind so many times?

This haircut was surely a form of bullying—just because I didn't look "boy enough" for him.

Again, Mama whispered, "You can stay home tomorrow, and you can stay home Friday, too. And guess what—fall break is next week, so that will give plenty of time for your hair to grow back."

"Watch and see, my dear, before you know it, your hair will be back." She kissed me on the forehead and said, "Go to bed, dear, and don't worry about a thing."

"But Mama, what about my eyes?" I asked.

Still holding me, she questioned, "Your eyes? What about your eyes?" That's when she took a second look and hollered,

"What the… who did this?"

"Dad," I answered.

"Why?" Mom asked.

"I don't know, Mama, but the ladies at the barbershop were saying how nice my eyelashes were. And on the way home, Dad stopped by the road and cut them off."

Mama closed her eyes and shook her head for a whole minute. I knew she was livid. But after that, she said, "Baby, go to bed and don't worry about a thing." Again, she kissed me on the forehead and watched me start up the stairs.

I'm grateful for Mama; she has always been my hero. Mom's love for me is unconditional, and I knew that. But I couldn't say the same thing about him. Something was different about him. He had issues that went deeper than me, and I thought I had problems.

I reached the top of the stairs but quickly tiptoed back down because I heard Mama's angry voice.

Mom was telling the man that he had taken things way too far and that he shouldn't have given me such a hideous haircut.

"What in hell possessed you to cut my child's eyelashes?" she argued.

That was the first time I had ever heard Mama use the word hell in that way. By this time, I was around the corner, listening.

She also said he was selfish and cold-hearted.

That night was terrifying, and I will never forget it. The man allowed Mama to vent, I guess, but then he slapped her hard.

That's when I walked into the kitchen.

Though I wouldn't stand up to him for myself, I had no problem standing up for my mom. The man had his hands around Mom's neck, bending her head backward and choking her over the kitchen sink. Mama was gasping for breath, trying to break free.

They didn't know I was standing there until I spoke up and said, "Dad, that's called bullying. Remember?"

Just a few nights ago, Mom, the man, my four sisters, and I watched a show about bullying. It was my sister Jean's school project. I liked it and learned a lot. The man didn't know what the movie was about; Mom just told him it would be a good movie to watch as a family.

The movie outlined the characteristics of a bully. The man was on my mind the entire time because he had always been my number one bully. That night, I used some of the words from the movie, speaking them directly to him. I knew it was risky—but it felt like my big day.

That's when everything exploded. He had just released his grip from Mom's neck—she collapsed to the floor, gasping for breath—and then he turned toward me. He walked over like a cowboy ready to draw his gun. I tried to look around him, hoping to help Mom, but he planted himself in front of me like the bully he was.

Without warning, he raised his massive hand and backhanded me. My body went flying across the room, and I hit my head against the counter. I probably didn't weigh more than sixty-five pounds. I lay there, bleeding, stunned.

Standing over me, he said, "Next time, think before you speak."

Then he left, storming out of the house. I could hear his car roaring down the street. My first thought was for Mom—I couldn't see her, couldn't help her. I wanted to scream, "Mom!" but nothing came out. Thankfully, she managed to reach me. Relief flooded me knowing she was okay.

The blood was pouring from my head. I lay there, weak and terrified. I knew I wasn't dead because I could feel it running down my face, but I didn't know if I was dying. Soon, the blood ran into my eyes and everywhere. Mama's hands shook like leaves in a storm as she pressed them against my head, trying to stop the bleeding. I'm sure she feared for my life just as much as I feared for hers.

And yet, the man, my tormentor was a deacon in the church, respected by the pastor and many others.

I knew if this had happened any other way, they would have rushed me to the hospital immediately. Maybe a little hair could have cushioned my head, but I had none. Mom worked tirelessly, trying to stop the bleeding. I wasn't in pain, not really but I wanted to fall asleep. Mama kept patting my face, whispering, "No, baby, don't sleep. Stay awake." The man, of course, didn't care if I lived or died.

If Mom hadn't been there, or if she had been rendered unconscious from his chokehold, he would have done nothing differently. He would have left me lying on the kitchen floor, bleeding, and walked away without a second thought. That was terrifying.

That night should have been a nightmare I could wake from, but it wasn't. Though the man had hurt me many times before, this was the first time he had raised his hand against me. Mom told me to pretend it never happened, that everything was under control now. "The devil jumped into him," she said. She believed it was the devil's fault—but I knew better.

The next day, when I saw the scarf Mom had wrapped around her neck, the memory hit me. Mom had often worn scarves before, just as a style choice, but now it all made sense. Dad had choked her then, too. Anger welled up inside me because Mom is such a sweet, caring person—someone who didn't deserve any of this.

I thought about talking to Uncle Joe, but I didn't. I decided not to tell anyone—not my sisters, not a soul. My head throbbed like I'd never felt before. This was what adults mean when they talk about a splitting headache. Every tiny movement made the pain worse, and all I wanted was to lie still. Mama stayed by my side all day, making sure I rested. Every few minutes, she checked on me, sometimes sitting quietly in my room just to comfort me. I clung to that—her presence was a balm in the middle of the chaos.

After several days, I could slowly walk around without the pounding pain, though I had to move stiffly to avoid it flaring again. I thought maybe, just maybe, the man would apologize. He could have easily killed me. His hands were massive, larger than most men's, but instead of remorse, he walked past me like I was nothing more than an unwanted picture on the wall. The man couldn't have missed the big white bandage covering most of my head, a reminder that he had nearly killed me. Mama had to change it two or three times a day.

I was told to say I'd run into a tree while riding my bike. That was Mama's lie, meant to keep the peace, never to cause harm. The man wasn't talking to Mama, and he certainly didn't have much to say to me. Well, to be honest, he had absolutely nothing to say. But of course, I said the stupidest thing possible.

"Dad," I asked, holding my head down so he could see the bandage, "is blood coming through my pad again?"

That was dumb. He didn't even glance at me. "Ask your Mama," he said, eyes glued to his shoes—or at least pretending to be. I figured maybe he expected me to apologize for being "disrespectful." So, after a couple of hours stewing, I went back and said, "Dad, will you please forgive me for disrespecting you? I'm sorry."

He finally looked at me and said, cold as ice, "Just know, if you should ever try that shit again, you won't be here to apologize."

"Yes, sir," I replied, and I bolted out of there as fast as I could.

The man is crazy. That wasn't at all what I was hoping to hear. After all that, he still didn't feel bad. He was still set to kill me. That's evil. How dare he blame me for what he did? He owes me an apology—whether he gives it or not.

CHAPTER 8

Looking Like a Fool

The man was so serious and self-dignified. He didn't smile much at all. And from the way he folded his lips, you would think he didn't have teeth.

One day, I asked Mama how she met the man. She said they met at a coffee shop. "So what attracted you to him?" I asked. "Was it the way he drank his coffee or the way he ate too many donuts?"

When she finished laughing, she said, "Both, I suppose." And we both laughed a bit more. I would guess nothing attracted her to him except his bank account. The man had money—I'd already done my research on that. He was left with a lot of money from the death of a family member. It was enough to put him on top of the mountain and get any woman of his choice—especially a struggling one.

Mama was a pretty lady, and she could have had any man she wanted, I would think. The man, on the other hand—not so much. If it wasn't his money, then I don't have the slightest clue what it was. It couldn't have been his personality, that's for sure.

The man used to just sit and watch me. But when he wasn't watching me, I was watching him. That's just the way he was.

He'd sit back and observe, and you'd wonder what he was thinking. I knew he was trying to figure out if I wanted to be a boy or a girl. But beyond that, he watched people in general.

He was the kind of person who would speak his mind, come push or shove—so don't push or shove. Deacon or no deacon, the man would give you a piece of his mind most of the time. But he should know that everybody isn't going to look over him… remember the lady at the barber shop?

I remember another time as well. This guy cut in front of the man at the checkout line. To be honest, the guy didn't even know the man was in line. Anyone would have assumed he was just standing there looking at the items on the end shelf. The guy was young, older than a college student, I would guess, but nowhere near the man's age.

Dad said, "Hey, buddy, whatever you are… you just cut in front of me as if I'm not standing here."

That was embarrassing. I would have known better than to say something like that.

The guy replied, "I'm sorry, I didn't know you were in line. But I noticed you addressed me as a 'whatever I am.'"

"Yes, I did," Dad said, "because I don't know what you are."

"Well," the guy said, "you might want to be careful how you choose your words, because you may have to say those same words to the kid standing there. And the way things are looking from my point of view, you might want to prepare yourself sooner rather than later."

Dad was left standing there looking like a fool. He expected nothing but an apology, but he got that—and more. And in my opinion, he deserved it.

I assume the guy saw me as a girl dressed as a boy. And that didn't bother me one bit, because that's exactly what I was.

If it were a fight, the guy definitely won. I knew the man was embarrassed because everyone standing around was tuned in.

He had it coming that day, and I bet he was too embarrassed to even mention it to Mama.

He reminded me of a judge, a mean one at that. The man wasn't the type to joke or laugh. And if he did laugh, it had to be a really good joke. Most people weren't comfortable around him either, because they couldn't figure him out. The only real friend he had was Mama.

He claimed to be a Christian, but sometimes he made me wonder what that word really meant.

Did I mention he has a twin? Well, he does. According to Uncle Joe, the man has a twin brother he stopped speaking to when they were nineteen years old. My father is almost forty-seven now, so that's been… what, too many years to count.

The man never speaks of his family, not even his mother or father. I wouldn't even know their names if it hadn't been for Uncle Joe. Mama mentioned a few things here and there, but never enough to piece together anything meaningful. It took Uncle Joe to tell the real story.

According to Uncle Joe, Dad's brother was once pulled over by the cops back in the day. He was so scared, he told them his name was Rusty Quick,, when his real name was Rodney Quick.

The man also has another brother named Reddy. I don't know him either. Uncle Joe said Reddy left home when he was seventeen, and they never saw him again. He's not dead or anything, though, because we receive cards and gifts from him every Christmas. And it never fails, the five gifts always arrive about three days after the New Year comes in. He never sends anything to Mom and Dad.

Uncle Reddy keeps up with all our names, ages, and birthdays. The ages are pretty easy since the four girls share the same birthday. I'm not sure who keeps him updated about us, but I would guess it's Uncle Joe.

Every year, Uncle Reddy asks us to send pictures back to his P.O. box—but we're not allowed to.

Between you and me, I sent him plenty of pictures of all of us last year. Mom and the man never knew. But if the man had found out that I disobeyed him like that, he would have skinned me alive. I made sure to cover my tracks by sending a letter, begging my uncle not to tell my parents.

The man is just cruel, because Uncle Reddy never did anything to him. Remember, he left home when he was seventeen. It was Uncle Rodney that the man had issues with. But still, he wanted nothing to do with Uncle Reddy either.

Evidently, Uncle Reddy knew from the start that his brother wanted no part of him. So there had to be more to the story. And the answer is simple, he didn't like the life Uncle Reddy chose to live. Point blank.

I've always wanted to meet Uncle Reddy. It's been on my dream list for as long as I can remember.

I mentioned that the man would have skinned me alive if he found out I shared our family photos with Uncle Reddy. But in reality, I've never received a whipping from either of my parents.

I've heard of children being whipped with belts or switches, but that never happened to me or my sisters. That's not counting the backhand slap I got from the man when I was about eight or nine.

Other than that, the man's eyes whipped me daily.

His eyes cut deeper than any belt or switch ever could. I felt so degraded when he looked at me and shook his head, like I was something disgusting.

I hope I didn't inherit anything from him. I think it's smart to look at the genes in your family, because they can explain a lot. But like I said, I'd rather none of my father's traits live in me.

Now, what if Uncle Reddy had a whole skeleton in his closet that led him to leave? Even a blind man could see there was more to the story. But he did what was best for him, and I'm not mad about that. If anything, I'm proud of him.

Speaking of genes, my grandmother on the man's side had triplets. So I guess that's how Mama ended up having quadruplets, it runs in the family, I suppose. That's one of the few things I know about the man's side, thanks to Uncle Joe.

Back to the story, the man spent two days in jail because of the lie his brother told, and he never spoke to him again. I don't know Rodney from Adam's cat, but I'm sure I would have called him Uncle Rodney if I had known him. According to Uncle Joe,

Uncle Rodney tried several times to apologize, but the man refused him every time. I can believe that.

It's sad that someone can be that cold-hearted. After all, they were brothers. People say young folks do foolish things, so why couldn't the man see it that way and just let it go? I know I would have.

You might wonder why Uncle Joe would tell a kid so much, but without him, I would have been in the dark about a lot. I'm smart enough to handle it. I think he sees something in me. I mean, I'm just as smart as some adults, at least smarter than the man, if you ask me.

I know one thing for sure: I would show love to my children. I'd make sure they knew I loved them, no matter how they looked.

My birth didn't bring the man joy at all; instead, it made his life miserable. Yes, trying to change a female's brain into a male's is more than hard, it's impossible.

The man never loved me. Let me correct that. He loved me when I was a baby, when I showed no signs of who I truly was.

But that's not real love. Still, I was treated with some form of love until I was about five. After that, all hell broke loose. That's when everything changed. He began to despise me, yet at the same time, he tried harder than ever to change me.

Truth be told, he only loved himself. Everything he did was about maintaining a certain image. Mom would try to reassure me that my dad loved me, but why would she need to convince me of that? I think she was really trying to convince herself.

Deep down, I felt like he could kill me, literally. That may sound harsh, but it's the truth.

I remember once standing in the bathroom, giving a long speech to a group of imaginary girls in the mirror. It was just me, hand on my hip, talking with a twist in my neck.

"I'm just like you—I'm a girl. I'm not a girl because of what's between my legs. I'm a girl because of what's in my head." I went on and on, speaking freely, boldly—like the girl I knew I was. It was a good speech, even if no one heard it but me.

It didn't take long before that little girl's personality started showing up around other people for real. Anyone with eyes could see it, and the man definitely did. And I wasn't a pleasant sight to him.

I can't count how many times he told me, "Man up and sound like a boy!"

But I wasn't trying to sound like a girl, and I wasn't trying to walk like one either. I tried—many times—to be what the man wanted me to be. I guess I didn't try hard enough, because at the end of the day, I was still me.

I would often catch him peeking at me… watching me. It felt creepy. I started walking stiff, trying to make sure my body didn't move in ways that would upset him. I'm sure I looked ridiculous.

Back then, I would have done anything to keep him from shaking his head at me. I hated that look. It stayed with me all day, making me feel small… making me feel worthless.

I guess I loved the man at one point—but it was a very short point. Or maybe I only respected him. Of course, I loved my mama, and I couldn't have loved her more.

At one time, I even felt sorry for the man, because something was clearly wrong with him. I thought maybe he wasn't loved as a child or something. I mean, if I could have changed myself, I would have done it for him in a heartbeat back then. I would have cut off my arms and legs and given them to him if that would have made him love me.

But after all that trying, and all that praying, for years, I would wake up every morning still me. They would have had a much easier journey if they had just cut the blame thing off and let me be. The thing was small anyway.

Did I mention that one of my sisters was born deaf? Because of that, we all learned sign language fluently. And signing has helped her tremendously. You see how they adjusted the situation so life could be easier for her. They should have done the same for me.

The youngest of the girls was born with a hole in her heart, but the doctors corrected it. You get my point. It could have been a simple, even enjoyable journey for all of us—but because of their religion and their God, they chose a completely different path.

Uncle Joe told me about my great-great-grandmother, who was born with one leg much shorter than the other, so she wore specially made shoes. The point I'm making is this: their conditions were understood and accommodated.

But what about me?

Oops—I was born with a penis…

Well, I guess I'm in this one by myself. Because… yes… because of the Bible.

CHAPTER 9

Afraid Of Gay Children

The man came up with an idea that he thought could "heal" me. Yeah… go him.

His brilliant idea was completely foolish. But it just goes to show how far people will go when they're desperate.

The man took me to be hypnotized. Yes, hypnotized.

That's the word. He didn't ask me if I wanted to go.

According to him, children speak only when spoken to. When grown folks are talking, or even thinking, children are to be silent.

I'll never forget it. Things couldn't have gotten any more ridiculous. I had seen stuff like this on TV, but never in real life.

Before we left, the man packed up his fishing gear right in front of Mama, as if we were actually going fishing. Fishing was something he used to do often, but not with me anymore.

It didn't take long for me to figure things out once we arrived at this little, funky-looking building. I started reading the posters on the half-painted walls. I sat there long enough to piece it all together. My heart started beating faster the more I understood.

The guy running the place must have been popular, because people were coming from everywhere. We waited while other parents went in first, to hand over their money.

Those parents were desperate, terrified of having gay children. They couldn't see that the man was running a scam. And I wouldn't doubt that most of them called themselves Christians.

There was only one con man working back there, taking people's money. After sitting there for two hours or more, you would think a miracle might have happened by then.

Finally, they called me to the back. "Jack B. Quick," someone announced. There I went again, like a sheep to the slaughter.

I had to lie down on an old couch, just like on TV, except this one looked like it belonged in a dumpster. The con man could have at least invested in something decent. But then again, I was tired from the long ride… not to mention the depressing waiting room.

Here we go.

I had to repeat after him: "I was born a boy, I will think like a boy, I will walk like a boy, I will conduct myself like a boy…"

and the nonsense went on and on. He just kept rattling off that same speech like he had it memorized for business purposes.

If that's all he was going to do, the man could have saved his money and just read the speech himself. But whether he admitted it or not, he knew the truth. He knew I was a girl—and that he was fighting a losing battle trying to turn me into something I wasn't.

The con man acted like he was putting me into a deep sleep. That's when I decided to be a little rebellious. Dad was sitting behind him, so he couldn't see me clearly.

"Just close your eyes for me," the con man said.

Instead, I blinked at him and kept staring.

"Go ahead… just close your eyes," he repeated.

I blinked about six quick times like I'd lost my mind and kept staring straight into his eyes. Honestly, it was kind of funny.

I knew he wasn't going to tell Dad—I mean, he didn't want to lose his money. So he kept going like I was following instructions.

"When I snap my fingers, open your eyes," he said.

My eyes were already open, but he snapped his fingers anyway. That's when I closed them.

"You can open your eyes now," he added.

I'm sure he was sick of me. But what the heck—he deserved it.

He tried to gently pull me up, but I leaned back on purpose, resisting just a little. In my mind, I was auditioning for a play.

I opened one eye and stuck my tongue out. I mean, what could he say or do… nothing.

"Is he okay?" the man asked.

The con man replied, "Oh yes, some tend to wake up slower than others, but that's a good sign."

What a joker.

When my dad turned around, I quickly shot the con man my middle finger. That was the icing on the cake.

He just stared at me like a fool. That probably had never happened in all his conning days. I'm sure I gave him something to talk about with his wife that night. I was glad to be of service.

Honestly, that was fun—and I'm pretty sure I got the part.

But here comes the funniest part of the day. Evidently, I had confused the con man with my "performance."

These were his exact words: "Just be patient with her and give her time, she will be fine."

Now that was hilarious. The con man accidentally called me a girl, the very thing he was being paid to erase.

The man looked at him and said, "You mean he."

"Excuse me?" the con man replied.

"You said she will be fine. You mean he," the man repeated.

"Oh yes, yes, yes," the con man stammered. "He will be fine."

Oh yeah… I bet his wife is still laughing about that one.

Yep, the con man was all mixed up. Truth be told, I think I hypnotized him that day. Didn't even know I had it in me.

But the man wasn't much better. He was so caught up in his reputation, so afraid of people thinking he had a gay son—that he couldn't see anything else. And the con man? He was just trying to fill his pockets by any means necessary.

Two peas in a pod.

The man stood there staring at me while I struggled to get off that old sofa. I fell back on it twice. He didn't like that, gave me that same mean look.

But shucks, I didn't mean to fall back. That thing felt like a bowl of jelly.

He was also trying to feel me out. I knew that too, like I'd just had surgery and everything was supposed to be fine.

If he could have read my mind, he would have heard me say, "Way to go, dummy! How much smarter can you get? We could've used that money for surgery."

Just imagine if we could read minds for real; it would be a war every day, all day. I know I'd be dead meat.

And I know exactly who would have killed me.

The man and the con man stepped away from me to talk in private. I gave it everything I had to hear what they were saying. I even closed my eyes and strained my ears. I heard the con man say, "Your son must take this very seriously." I heard that.

And I thought to myself: sure, crook, shift the blame onto the kid. How could adults be so ignorant? I was barely a pre-teen, and I already knew this man was a crook.

The con man handed the man what looked like a part of a plant. He told him to bury it somewhere; I couldn't figure that part out.

But when we walked out, I decided to shoot the con man my middle finger one more time. I made sure I was going to be in his conversation that night. I'm sure he thought awful things about me as a kid, but who cares?

I should write a book entitled When Christians Get Desperate. This is the kind of stuff they do. The head deacon at that, the one who tells everybody else what to do.

Right before we pulled off, the man told me never to mention this day to Mom. I said, "Okay." Then he added, "You know, Jack, that cost me some hard-earned money in there, and I hope you take it seriously." And again, I said, "Okay."

We rode all the way home in silence. That would have been the perfect time for a father-to-son talk, but nope, that didn't happen. And neither did anything happen in that creepy-looking building. Let me rephrase that… Today the man wasted gas, he wasted time, and he wasted plenty of money.

That's the craziest thing ever, the man never had one conversation with me about how I felt. I just can't get over that. He never said, "Jack, you do enjoy being a boy or something like that?" After all, he was a grown man… and grown folks can say whatever the hell they want.

I don't know what he expected me to do. Why would I take something seriously that I didn't ask for? Something he didn't even bother to explain to me. I had to figure it out myself!

I'm not a boy, don't want to be a boy, so there you have it! That's exactly what I was screaming to him in my head.

Who in the hell raised you, man? Coyotes?! That's more of what I was screaming inside my head.

If I can't change my own brain, then how could somebody else magically do it? This is who I am, nut bucket! That's what was going around in my head.

Shortly after we got home, I saw the man digging a hole in the backyard, and he dropped that thing inside. He stood there for a moment, then covered the hole up. Wow, I wondered if that was in the Bible.

The next day at school, I couldn't wait to lay eyes on Robert L. Northerner, the guy I'd secretly admired since fourth grade.

CHAPTER 10

The Day I Met Rj

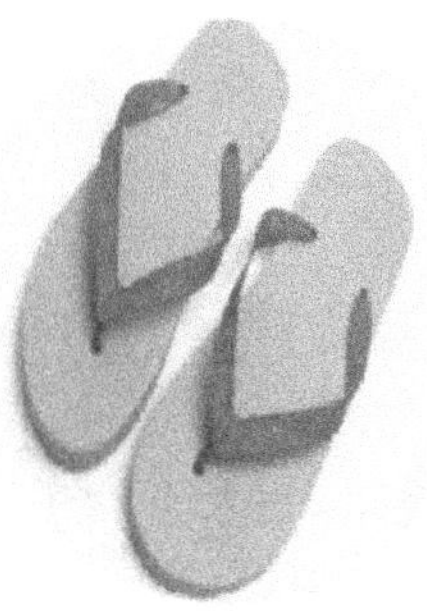

I made it to middle school alive, and to my surprise, I found RJ! The name RJ sounds like a boy's name, but she was in no way a boy. She was a girl, just like me—minus the penis, of course. RJ and I would talk and laugh forever about everything. She called me Jackie, not Jack. That was cool. I liked the name Jackie.

When I looked in the mirror, I didn't see a boy. I saw a girl with a boy's haircut. I'd think to myself, if only I were older, I'd let my hair grow out like that girl Jada. It would be long and pretty, just like hers. Of course, I'd have to move to another world, because the man would still kill me… though he's so god-like.

If I were older, I'd ask him, where was your god when you carried me to be hypnotized? Actually, I had a long list of questions.

I could never connect the dots of Christianity. The man was just as confused as the book he read. According to him, God is not the author of confusion. Really? Then why was he so confused?

I don't know who inspired the book, but I do know it couldn't have been an all-knowing, all-loving God. It would be pretty dumb of such a being to send a message in the form of a text, causing nothing but fights, debates, and just plain confusion. I mean, that's what the Bible has done. Everybody thinks they are right and the other person is wrong when it comes to the scriptures.

If that's not confusion, I don't know what is. And with that being said, who should be blamed for the fights? My point exactly.

Mama purchased something off Amazon, but she couldn't put the "blame thing" together because the instructions were confusing. She then looked at the reviews… which she should have done beforehand. But everyone was complaining about the instructions. So, with that being said, who's to blame for the confusion? The only difference in this scenario and that of the Bible is that the Amazon person can be tracked down and fix the situation, but the God of the Bible cannot. Well, He hasn't so far. And this can be applied to all the other thousands of religions and gods.

The day I met RJ was the same day I wore my flip-flops to school. Mama didn't like those shoes, so she threw them away, but I found them. She said she didn't like the way the flip-flops made me walk. I had a little butt on me; not a lot, but enough that Mama probably would have changed it if she could. If the man wasn't always in Mama's ear, she would have been willing to talk to me about me. But he's always working to indoctrinate her with his way of thinking, and I was working to indoctrinate her too.

This particular day, RJ was walking behind me in the crowded hallway and accidentally stepped on the back of my flip-flop, causing it to break between my toes. She felt really bad and said she was so sorry. While she was being apologetic, my eyes were glued to my toes wiggling free of the strap. Then, for some reason, it tickled me silly, and I burst out laughing. RJ paused, seeing me laughing, and she started laughing too. That was the beginning of our friendship.

To my surprise, she had an extra pair of flip-flops in her locker that fit me perfectly. Her flip-flops were prettier than mine. I was glad the accident happened—and plus, she became my best friend that day.

RJ wore flip-flops the next day too, and she had her toenails polished in a beautiful pink color—my favorite. Her toes were so pretty, I wished so badly that I could polish my toenails too. I'd polish them pink, just like hers.

She and I clicked instantly, but before the day was over, she asked the big question: "Are you really a girl, or are you really a boy? Because you look like a girl." I happily responded, "I'm a girl everywhere… except there," and I kind of looked down at myself. I had to explain to her about my birth, how I was born with the penis thing. I said something funny about it, and we laughed all the way down the hallway. I had never laughed so much at school.

The closest laughs I usually got were the students laughing at me. But that day, a heavy weight lifted off my shoulders. For the first time in my life, I was excited about going to school.

One day, RJ and I talked more about the penis I was born with, but this time, she wanted to see it. I had no problem letting her. After all, it wasn't anything I wanted. Then she wanted to touch it. That was fine too. Using her pencil, she lifted it and flipped it around here and there as if she was dissecting a worm, something she was usually afraid of. Every time she flipped it, she'd jump back, and we would laugh so hard.

"Wow," she said, "this is what they look like in real life?"

And we laughed even more. We were both so happy to have each other. After that, she never asked to see it again.

RJ was in love with a boy at school named Jackson. Jackson wasn't mean to her, but he never gave her the time of day.

He didn't know that she almost worshipped the ground he walked on. He was quiet and only spoke when he had something to say. He didn't start any trouble; he simply stayed to himself. He seemed like a pretty good dude. He didn't seem to care what other people were doing or thinking.

On the other hand, I was crazy about this guy named Robert, Robert L. Northerner. I was just another boy to him who looked like a girl, I suppose. To be honest, I don't know if he'd ever noticed me at all.

But I was a girl—a girl with a boy piece, that's all.

I would daydream about Robert quite often. Imagination can be a good thing, I think. Sometimes it's the only way to get the things you want in life. So, I just go ahead and daydream.

I don't know how I would have made it without RJ; she was the only one interested in hearing about me and how I felt. It felt so good to finally talk to someone about me for a change.

She told people she was my girlfriend so I wouldn't be picked on so badly. But they still picked on me because of it. One way or another, I was going to get picked on. Still, it was so much better having a friend. She said she would protect me. I didn't really understand what she meant by that. RJ was three times a girl, not because she was fat, but because she was extra girly. Her weight didn't bother me in the least.

Everybody said I walked like a girl. But I didn't know any other way to walk. And after all, that's what I was. I guess I could try to "pimp walk" or something, you know, put one foot ahead like a leader and drag the other. Then you've got to swing your arms around like a monkey. Nope, I don't think so. I'd be exhausted by the end of the day.

My folks made sure I dressed like a boy from head to toe. I would take off those old boy shoes and put on my flippers every chance I got. I had to wear plaid-looking shirts buttoned all the way up to the neck. It's embarrassing just thinking about it.

People often looked down on RJ because she was overweight. Sometimes students would ask me why I liked "that fat white girl." Every time, I'd respond, "Fat?" (looking puzzled).

"I've never noticed that." I made that line up just so I'd have something ready when people came at me with that nonsense.

Of course, they'd look at me like I was crazy every time. And yes, RJ was fat, but she was also pretty. People couldn't see her beauty because they were too focused on her weight, but I chose to see her differently.

I'm sure people at school asked RJ why she hung out with someone like me, but we never shared those negative comments with each other. I didn't want to weigh her down with all that foolish talk, and I guess she felt the same about me.

CHAPTER 11

Bruce Makes Rj Cry

Rj was, without a doubt, my best friend. Sometimes I even called her my angel.

One Friday morning, I found my angel standing at her locker, crying. It crushed me to see her like that. RJ was a girly girl, but not the kind you'd catch crying. I kept asking her what was wrong, but she only shook her head. Thankfully, a new girl standing nearby stuttered, "Th-that boy Bruce… he was pushing her and calling her fat names."

Even through the stutter, I knew exactly who she meant. Bruce was one of the daily bullies at that school, except that day, he messed with the wrong person. My whole body filled with rage.

RJ looked at me, tears streaming down her cheeks, shaking her head. I knew what she was thinking: Don't do anything stupid.

I looked at the new girl, and she pointed toward the lunchroom. I took off running as fast as I could. I spotted Bruce from a distance, and without thinking, I ran straight into him, shoving him as hard as I could. He stumbled back like a drunk man, crashing over several chairs.

Bruce yelled, "Faggot, you're dead meat now!" But his words only made me stronger. There wasn't a fearful bone in my body. I kept moving toward him as he struggled to get up. In my deepest voice, I said, "Why did you hurt my angel?"

Still struggling to get up, he said what damn angel? Oh... that fat white girl."

By the time the words "white girl" left his mouth, I was already on him. I lit into him with my fists, over and over again.

My folks named me Jack, but in that moment, I felt like I had turned into Jack Johnson. I didn't give him a chance to recover. I kept throwing punches, hard, fast, nonstop.

All I could see in my mind was RJ crying. The more I saw her face, the harder I hit. I didn't miss a beat.

Mr. Andy, my science teacher, struggled to pull me off that boy. I had always felt like a bolt of lightning, and that day, I proved it. My last name was Quick, so hey, it fit.

Bruce was bleeding from the mouth and head, but I still wasn't done. I broke free from Mr. Andy and got in two or three more licks. I don't know what came over me that day, but it was something different, something strong. RJ was too kind of a person to be treated like that.

Bruce's face was messed up, and I was proud to be the one who did it.

Word spread fast: Jack walked like a girl, but he beat Bruce down like a man.

Here's the thing, Bruce was known as a bully at school. He was always in trouble and would curse out a teacher in a heartbeat.

Most of the students were afraid of him… including me.

I was suspended for ten days after the fight, but that was fine. There wasn't a teacher who cared much for Bruce anyway.

Strangely, neither his mother nor his father came to the school to ask about what happened. I could have been in serious trouble with the law, his face was that messed up. I don't know why no charges were filed against me, but they weren't. Two months passed, and I still hadn't heard anything.

When Bruce came back to school, his face was still marked up from the fight. Most of the teachers probably figured he had it coming. Bruce gave everyone problems.

And truth be told, I think Mr. Andy could've pulled me off him a lot sooner—kept me from going back for that second round. But he didn't.

He knew exactly what he was doing.

My mom gave me a long talk about how there are better ways to settle problems, and fighting isn't one of them.

I was a little scared to go back to school, thinking Bruce might try to beat me down. I had already planned it out in my head, if he did, I'd just picture RJ standing there crying, and I'd beat him down all over again. But to my surprise, he showed me nothing but respect, just like everyone else after that.

If they only knew, I didn't really know how to fight like that. I was just as surprised as anyone about what happened. But I do know one thing: no one ever picked on RJ again. When we walked by, students stepped aside. Yep… pretty strange. And Bruce was never the school bully again, either.

RJ came home with me quite often. At first, my parents got excited because they thought I had gotten myself a girlfriend. They didn't care if she was fat, white, black, or green—just as long as she was a she. It didn't take long for them to realize RJ was just my friend. Sometimes I'd call her RJ, and other times, I'd call her my angel.

Mom questioned me about that once, and I said, "Oh Mom, it stands for friend."

My angel would bring extra clothes in her bag so I could prance around in them. We had the best time together. She'd do my makeup, and we'd play school, I was always the teacher.

Mama would hear us carrying on and yell, "What are y'all doing up there?" and I'd holler back, "Just playing a game, Mom!"

My angel's clothes were way too big for me, but that didn't matter. We made it work. I loved the feeling of wearing pretty things instead of those old blue jeans and shirts I had to wear every day. I wanted to at least tie my T-shirt to the side like the other girls at school—and with RJ, I got to do all that and more.

CHAPTER 12

Making a Difference

A few weeks after the fight, I started thinking about the girl who told me about Bruce Moose. I remembered how she stuttered through every word. I wondered if she had any friends. I knew what it felt like not to have one. So, I made it my business to watch her, sometimes even follow her.

At lunch, she sat outside in the same spot, always by herself. During school breaks, I'd see her alone, reading a book or something. She was always alone. And she walked with her head down, just like I used to.

I brought RJ in on my little investigation. She knew that lonely feeling too. After watching this girl for a whole week, we both knew, she was hurting from it.

We decided to try to be her friend.

One day at lunch, I walked by her with my skates in my hand and politely sat down on the bench beside her. I started messing with my shoestring, pretending to fight with this crazy knot. I didn't say anything at first, just sat there, tussling with it. She didn't say a word either. After a few minutes, I finally said, "Has this ever happened to you?"

She looked at me and gave a small smile.

I kept going. "This is crazy. My mom is going to kill me. She told me not to tie them like this again."

She still didn't say anything. She'd glance at me every now and then, but that was it. I was hoping she'd offer to help—but she didn't. So I kept pretending to struggle.

Finally, I asked, "Do you have fingernails? Mine are too short."

She looked down at her nails and nodded. "Yes."

"Oh great," I said. "Will you help me?"

So we sat there together, working to get both skates unknotted. While we worked, I asked her if she knew how to skate.

She nodded again. "Yes."

I already knew why she didn't want to talk.

I was so glad she spoke up for RJ that day when Bruce was picking on her.

"Can you skate really good, or just a little good?" I asked.

She laughed a little.

“Well,” I said, like she had asked me, “I don’t like bragging about myself, but I think I can skate pretty good.”

She laughed a little more. Finally, she got my shoestring loose. “Thanks a lot,” I said. “Can you do this one too? I’m having a hard time.”

She started working on the other one and got it loose pretty fast.

“Wow,” I said, “I need to grow my nails a little.”

After putting on my skates, I said, “Can you do this?” and I started skating backward.

She smiled and nodded.

“Okay then,” I said, “can you do this?” I did a little spin, and she nodded again. “What about this?”

That time, I fell.

I could tell I was getting somewhere with her. After a few rounds of laughing, I finally asked her name.

She pulled out a piece of paper and wrote, Blossom.

“Blossom, that’s a neat name,” I said. “Well, Blossom, my name is Jackie. Nice to meet you. One more question… do you talk?”

This time, she wrote, I can talk, but I stutter really badly, so I prefer writing or signing.

“I love signing!” I said, all excited. “My sister is deaf, so we talk with her all the time using sign language.”

Blossom lit up. She started signing to me, and we talked until the bell rang. I wasn't even ready to go.

The next day at lunch, I introduced Blossom to RJ, and they clicked right away. RJ knew how to sign too, so everything just flowed.

Blossom was happy, but she started trying to buy our friendship by giving us things. RJ and I both talked to her about it and explained that we were her friends, and our friendship was free. It didn't take long for her to believe us.

The three of us went skating all the time, and it was nothing but pure fun. It felt like we had known Blossom forever. She lived with her mother and had never really had a true friend before.

RJ came up with a brilliant idea, to start a friendship club and call it A.F.F., which stood for "A Friend Forever." We started greeting each other by saying, "Friend." Just like that, we had a club.

It became our thing to look around school for anyone who didn't have friends. We'd become their friend first, then introduce them to the club.

Come to find out, there were a lot of people without friends. In that first month, we found five new ones, not counting Blossom. That made eight of us.

RJ, being as creative as she was, handmade these really cute bracelets for all of us to represent our friendship.

CHAPTER 13

Uncle Joe Spills The Tea

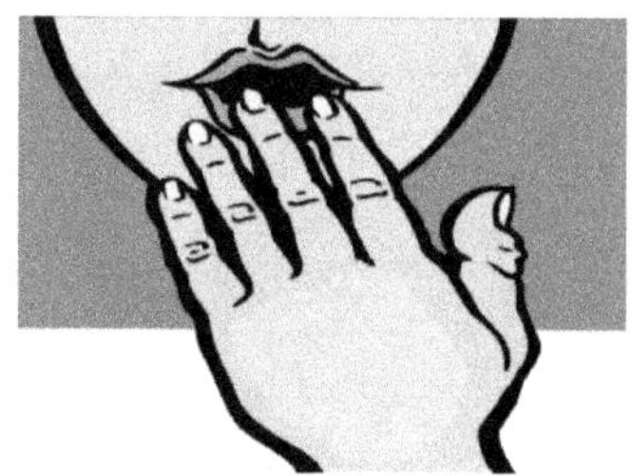

One day, Mama and I were laughing our butts off watching Family Feud. Then the show was suddenly interrupted with breaking news. A high school boy had tried to take his own life because he didn't know how to deal with being gay. It was a sad story. The boy was still hanging on, and his family didn't know if he was going to make it.

Mama sat there, making it her business not to look my way, but I saw her eyes fill with tears. I knew she was thinking about me.

You'd think that would've been a lightbulb moment for her, but nope. In her mind, she couldn't change the Bible. It plainly said that gays were not acceptable to God and should be killed. I remembered the days when Dad would make me write that whole page over and over, just to be sure I read that one particular scripture.

While I was watching Mama, Uncle Joe was standing in the doorway behind us. "That's sad," he said.

I turned around and yelled, "Hey, Uncle Joe!" He was the best uncle ever. I was always excited to see him.

Mama didn't even speak to him. She just rushed out of the room. Normally, she would've been happy to see her brother.

Uncle Joe came in and sat down on the sofa, looking like he had something on his mind. When he finally spoke, I could tell, this wasn't just small talk.

He glanced over his shoulder, then leaned in a little closer. "Jack," he said, "I'm going to tell you something I've never told a soul. I know what you're going through."

I froze as he continued.

"I've hidden the real me for over forty years," he said. "I was born male, but I've always been attracted to the same sex. Not the American way, right?"

I swear, I almost fell backwards when he said that.

"But you, my dear," he went on, "were born female with male organs. Meaning, Jack… you are transgender."

"A transgender?" I questioned with my eyes alone. But he kept going, answering as if I had asked out loud.

"Transgender people have a gender expression that differs from the sex they were assigned at birth. Jack, you are not alone. Not at all. There are millions of people just like you."

Wow… that was new information. I had never heard that before. How did he know so much? Had he been talking to Mama or somebody? No, no, no. Mama would never have a conversation like that.

"You see, Jack," he said, glancing upward, "we can either make lemonade out of these lemons or live our lives in sadness. I made the mistake of living mine that way. Don't do what I've done. People thought I was happy, and that's exactly what I wanted them to think. I hid behind the Bible most of my life, afraid to follow my heart. I've been preaching from a book that left me unhappy… a book that's nothing less than the author of confusion. But because the majority accepted it, I thought I should too."

Oh man… Uncle Joe was saying my thoughts out loud.

I couldn't believe the words coming out of his mouth. Was he really saying he didn't believe in the Bible? Then why was he still playing the role of a pastor? I was too shocked to ask—and I didn't want to sound stupid either. After all, he was trusting me with something big. But truth be told, I felt like I'd been blown away by the wind. I couldn't even open my mouth for hours after he left.

Uncle Joe didn't walk like a woman. He didn't talk like one, and he didn't want to be one. But he admitted he was attracted to the same sex. Who would've ever thought?

My mother would probably die if she knew.

“There was this one guy who wanted me as his partner,” he said. “And I wanted him just the same—maybe even more. But I turned him down over and over until he finally gave up. I was determined to do what people called ‘the right thing.’ I wanted to obey God and respect the Bible. But I never forgot Reagan. I would just daydream about him. That was the only place I felt happy.”

When Uncle Joe mentioned daydreaming, my eyes lit up. I thought about how I had been using that same escape.

“I made a choice, Jack,” he said. “I didn’t want the embarrassment, and I didn’t want to bring grief to my family. So I chose to be unhappy just to make everyone else comfortable. I’m not telling you this so you can go and let the cat out of the bag, not yet. You’re still depending on your family for everything.

“It’s sad, but news like this makes people lose their minds. They think it’s right to disown their own family just because someone is different. But you have time to prepare yourself. I’m just saying, be strong. Don’t let anyone rob you of your happiness. Be proud of who you are. Don’t be ashamed.”

He paused, then went on.

“I’ve spent time with beautiful, respectful women in my life. I kept trying to become who people thought I was—or who I was supposed to be. But nothing changed, Jack. I am who I am, and that’s it.

"I've questioned and pleaded with the God of the Bible. I've said so many times, 'God, please… please make me into the person you want me to be.' I prayed for over forty years. You'd think He would have heard me. You'd think something would have changed. But nothing did. Because He wasn't there… it's all just a story."

Oops… he lost me again.

Was he really saying there is no God? I mean, he said it as plain as the nose on my face—but did he really mean that? I wasn't about to mess this moment up, so I kept that question to myself for another time.

"It's a journey, Jack," he said, "but don't make it harder than it has to be. If I could do it all over again, I would stand up for who I am."

"And Jack," he added, leaning in a little closer, "don't be too surprised when you hear me give a speech in church about coming out. I'm not dead yet, I've got a lot more living to do.

"If I get one more chance at happiness, I'm taking it. I refuse to give my family every ounce of me while getting nothing in return. We only get one life."

"The guy you were talking about," I asked, "is he still around? I mean… do you ever see him?"

"Yes," he said. "Matter of fact, he comes to our church every Sunday now. I don't know what's going on in his head—he just sits, listens, and leaves. But I know I'm still in love with him. And if he asks me one more time… I'm saying yes."

He took a breath, then softened his voice.

"But enough about me. Some things we have to experience for ourselves, but there's also so much we can learn from others.

Your mom and dad may never understand you, because religion has limited the way they think. They may cause you a lot of pain… but don't take it to heart. Charge it to their ignorance, not their love.

"I'm telling you all this because if someone had told me what I'm telling you now, back when I was young… my life wouldn't have been filled with so much sadness and shame."

CHAPTER 14

My Eighth-Grade Dance

I'll never forget the eighth-grade dance—I wanted to go so badly. I imagined how it would feel to dress like the girl I am and actually be there. I imagined it so much… it ended up happening.

It started like this. My sister Jean let someone put a tattoo on her arm, and I happened to see it. Knowing Mama and the man would be furious if they found out, she begged me, with tears in her eyes, not to tell. I wasn't planning on telling anyway.

She quickly made a deal. If I kept quiet, she'd let me wear her outfit to the dance. That couldn't have come at a better time. So she helped me get dressed, and so kindly did my makeup too. I felt like a million bucks. I was beautiful.

When we were done, I looked just like her. The four of them looked so much alike, it was almost unreal. Sometimes even I got them confused, Da'Jean, Regina, La'ren, and of course, Jean.

They loved tricking teachers at school so much that it became mandatory for them to wear name tags every day. But even then, they'd still switch them around sometimes. Jean thought she was a comedian—she wasn't. She could be a little funny now and then, but not laugh-until-you-cry funny like RJ.

So I made it to the dance, and at first, nothing had ever felt better. But let me tell you, nothing had ever felt worse either.

Somewhere along the way, it became clear I had made the biggest mistake of my life. My excitement took a sharp turn. I felt like I'd been stripped naked and hung up in the school cafeteria for everyone to see.

Before that shift, though, a lot of boys wanted to dance with me, except for Robert Northerner. They really thought I was one of the girls; they just didn't know which one.

Over and over, they'd ask, "Which one are you?" and I'd laugh and say, "I can't tell ya."

I was actually having fun.

Then Larry Snowbell quickly guessed that I was Jean.

I saw Robert playing games in the game area, but he never came out onto the dance floor. Midway through the dance, I spotted the worst face ever… the man. My heart dropped to the floor, and I felt sick enough to throw up. He had that mean face on, Mama wasn't with him. I knew she had to be in the car.

Long story short, Jean had ratted me out. I couldn't understand why she would do that after the tattoo deal.

Little did I know, Jean had set me up to fail, yep, all on purpose. The tattoo was fake! All she had to do was wipe it off with a damp cloth. I should have known, but I was too caught up in my dream. I promised myself I'd never speak to her again.

The man couldn't figure out where I was, even though he was standing right in front of me. I continued dancing with my head down. But before I knew it, he had snatched me up under my arm and escorted me out. I was beyond embarrassed.

The school probably knew my folks, so the smart ones would figure out the blame game quickly. The man practically shoved me into the car. Mama didn't say a word, but I knew she was very disappointed in me. I felt awful for letting her down.

"And don't get in here trying to shift lies onto someone else just to cover your butt," the man argued. "There's no need to lie about your sister, Jack; she told us all about your ungodly act."

I hadn't said a word about my sister—but he was right, there was no need.

"Do you know you're going to burn in hell because of this mess? Hell is not a place you want to be, Jack! Do you want to go to hell?"

I didn't answer, so he shouted again, "Do you want to go to hell?"

"No, sir," I said.

"Then you better cut this nonsense out, and cut it out right now! You don't have to be like this, and you know it. This is something you're making up in your head, letting the devil have his way with your mind. You better start praying this away. It's nothing but the spirit of the devil, and you're letting it toss you around like a rag doll."

Mama handed me a pair of jeans and a T-shirt. She looked like she wanted to cry, even though she didn't say a word.

I can't even explain how low I felt. I probably stank to my mama now. I already felt like nothing to the man, but now, I felt like nothing to her too. This was the last straw. I had never gone this far before, and I knew it would never be forgotten. If I had the power, I would've disappeared and never come back.

If I had been older, I would've left home like Dad's brother and never returned. That way, I wouldn't have to put Mama through this. But I had nowhere to go, and I wasn't old enough to do anything. Tears streamed down my face. I felt like crawling into a hole.

Dark thoughts started creeping in ways I could just… disappear. I thought about Mama's blood pressure pills sitting in the house. My mind started telling me that if I took all of them, everything would just stop, and nobody would have to worry about me anymore. The idea began to feel real, almost like a plan, as the man kept fussing all the way home. By the time we pulled into the yard, my thoughts had gotten heavy and dangerous.

When we got inside, Mama's pills were sitting right there on the counter. She must've taken one before we left for the school. I figured after everything that happened, her blood pressure probably went up.

Walking through the kitchen on the way to my room, I quickly grabbed the pill bottle and made my way up the stairs. I passed by Jean on my way up. I really don't think she realized how serious this was. She had on a sleeveless shirt, wiping her arm with a washcloth, letting me know it was fake.

I didn't give a second thought to what I was about to do. Tears streamed down my face as I sat on my bed, staring at what I held in my hands. I just wanted it to be over.

And as far as me going to hell, I didn't even believe there was a hell, no more than the one I felt I was already living in. My only plan was to get out of it as soon as possible.

I took all the pills, and I lay my back waiting for death.

The next thing I remember was waking up. I didn't know what had happened. But I quickly realized I was still here—still in the same place I didn't want to be. I later learned I had already been in the hospital for four days.

Things felt like they were only going to get worse. Part of me had already started thinking about what I would do differently next time.

I kept my eyes closed, even though I was aware of everything around me. People came in and out, family, and folks I didn't even know. Everyone whispered, trying not to wake me.

Jean came in like I was already gone. She stood over me crying and apologizing, but it didn't change anything for me. I still wanted out.

I stayed in that hospital for another week. I barely moved, barely spoke. My body felt heavy, like it didn't belong to me anymore.

Mama cried every time she entered the room, while the man tried to comfort her. She believed it was her fault. I wanted to tell the man, "Shut the hell up." Why couldn't they just let me die? Then it wouldn't be anyone's fault. I knew Mom would cry for days, but eventually, she would realize that my dying was for the best.

Because of my illness, the doctor said no family member needed to stay overnight or all day in the room with me because it could make things worse. He was right on that part. He assured them that I would be well taken care of. Being that I was in intensive care, they would be watching me at all times…

That was creepy, sounds like my folks' so-called God.

The doctor said I was depressed, and he prescribed me some pills that were too small to see with the naked eye. I still managed to spit them out when the coast was clear.

I stayed with my eyes closed for the next two weeks at home. Mama and the man were still waiting on God to heal me from being gay and stupid. They didn't even know I wasn't gay.

Mama, with her smart brain, figured out that I wasn't swallowing the pills, so she made me swallow them every time in front of her. After taking the pills for a few days, I began to feel better. I still wanted to be dead. My arms weren't as heavy, and my legs were feeling better too—but who cared?

I kept wondering why I hadn't heard from RJ. I later found out that the man gave her excuses every time she stopped by. He said RJ was bad company and that I needed to leave her alone.

That made me so mad. I knew that was not going to happen as long as I was living, because RJ was my true friend.

Here's the thing, I knew I didn't wake up one day and choose whether I wanted to be a boy or a girl. Who does? Really… did you? Of course not. You and I both know it wasn't about making a choice. It was already there, set in concrete in our brains at birth, waiting to spring forth. Things had to finish developing, of course—just like everything else we're born with. In fact, we didn't know much of anything when we were born.

But let the truth be told, people should be free to live their lives however they want, and it shouldn't matter if you were born a certain way or not. It shouldn't matter if you chose or not, as long as you are not harming anyone.

That's just how I feel about it.

CHAPTER 15

Believing The Lies

My folks came to believe, with the help of a liar, that I was severely depressed. I wasn't just depressed anymore; I was officially severely depressed and "acting out." Wow… I was a severely depressed actor. Yep, acting like I wanted to be a girl, they said. To be honest, I had every right to be severely depressed.

My parents had a habit of believing preachers, especially the "God said" kind. You know the ones… always claiming God told them something about you. They make sure to announce it before the congregation too, like God personally pulled them aside and whispered your business in their ear. Makes them look important, I suppose.

I mean really, if God is talking like that for real, then they should know where some of those missing children are…the ones on milk cartons and cereal boxes.

Or better yet, they should go to hospitals and nursing homes and heal people—like they claim they're doing within the four walls of their churches.

The psychiatrist was very nice and tried to act like she was my friend. She didn't know I was ten steps ahead of her—unlike my folks. She wanted me to tell her things about myself—what I liked doing, my favorite show, my favorite place, and so on.

There wasn't much to tell, really, nothing beyond the fact that I was born with a penis and didn't want it, and that the man had a problem and was trying to indoctrinate my mom with stuff from the Bible.

But of course… she didn't ask about any of that.

CHAPTER 16

Uncle Joe's Announcement

This was sure to be the best Sunday of all. I noticed Uncle Joe talking to a man at church, and I couldn't help but wonder—was he the guy? Ever since Uncle Joe told me about the love of his life, I'd been watching, wondering, trying to figure it out. I mean, where did the guy sit every Sunday? Uncle Joe said he sat in the same seat every week, but he never said where.

I hated that my uncle had been unhappy for so many years.

I'll be eighteen in a little while… maybe he and I could talk more then, I thought.

I was standing in the hallway when Uncle Joe walked up and said, "Hey, Jack, you ready?"

"Ready for what?" I asked.

He quickly slipped a yellow sticky note into my hand and kept walking. Before I even looked at it, I watched him until he turned into the sanctuary. He had a bounce in his step—I'd call it a happy walk.

I unfolded the note, thinking it was just a piece of trash. But that "trash" had four important words written on it: my coming-out day.

It didn't take long for the light to come on in my head. This was going to be my uncle's big day. The opportunity had finally presented itself, and Uncle Joe was about to let the cat out of the bag.

I rushed to the sanctuary as fast as I could. I don't even know why I was so nervous—but I was shaking like a leaf on a tree. I made sure the man was sitting with Mom, because she was going to need him for real this time. I found an end seat two rows behind them… and I was ready to watch the show.

After the singing, Uncle Joe stepped to the pulpit and greeted everyone as usual. Then he started telling a very interesting story about being judgmental. I don't know about anybody else, but that was a story to be remembered.

Then he began to tell another story. I knew this one was his.

He said he wanted to tell a story about three bodies. One called "Truelove," one called "Family," and the third called "I."

"I" loved two bodies dearly—"Family" and "Truelove." But "Family" didn't like "Truelove," even though "I" was in love with "Truelove."

"I" had to make a choice between "Family" and "Truelove."

Uncle Joe paused and said, "Church, make sure this service is recorded today, because it's going to make headlines." Then he repeated himself like some preachers do, "Somebody say headlines. I need you to listen closely—I don't want anyone falling behind on this story."

They didn't know where Uncle Joe was going with it… but I did. I was so excited I could have peed in my pants.

"'I' made his choice," Uncle Joe continued, "and he canceled out 'Truelove' in order to keep 'Family.'"

The church let out that long, sad "ohhh" sound.

"So 'Family' went on for many years, doing what they do and enjoying their lives. But 'I' was never happy, because 'I' had canceled out 'Truelove' for the sake of 'Family.'"

"Oh, but the story doesn't end there," Uncle Joe said. "Today, 'I,' after many years, has the opportunity to have 'Truelove' again. And this time, 'I' has decided that if 'Family' can't accept 'Truelove,' then too bad."

Then he said, "Now church, I said all that to say this… I am the 'I' in the story. And I have decided to be with 'Truelove' for the rest of my life—regardless of 'Family.'"

Uncle Joe grabbed his coat and put it on slowly. He picked up his Bible and laid it on the altar.

His last words were, "I feel like a man who thought he had life in prison… until one day he heard a knock on his door, and the guard said, 'You can go now. You are free.'"

Uncle Joe stepped down from the pulpit and said, "Come forth, my Truelove."

A man stood up, waved his hand, and walked toward him. When he reached Uncle Joe, he kissed him on each cheek. Uncle Joe looped his arm through his Truelove's arm, and together they proudly walked out of the church.

Believe me when I say over half the church was clapping.

Mama literally fainted—the man had to carry her out. I don't know what else happened inside, because I got out of there. I wanted to see them ride off together.

And I did.

I watched Uncle Joe and his Truelove ride away in a limousine.

CHAPTER 17

Mama's Love

It's been over a month, and Mama still hasn't been to a church of any kind. She's been sad a lot… maybe even depressed. And the man doesn't help the situation at all. I don't know if she will ever get over the fact that her brother is gay.

The man started going to a church around the corner, and somehow, he became the head deacon there too. He made the girls go every Sunday. He didn't invite me at all…

I'm surprised he hasn't forced Mama to go.

Mama and Uncle Joe finally started talking on the phone again, but he hadn't come over to see her—not even once.

The man wanted nothing to do with Uncle Joe and couldn't stand to hear his name.

"Why do you even waste your time talking to that faggot?" he said.

"Because he's my brother," Mama responded.

"Well, your brother is somewhere hunching a man."

"Randy, he's an adult, and he's free to make his own choices."

"The Bible speaks against it, you know," the man added.

"Yes, it does, and it also speaks against you choking me. But how many times have you done that?"

"You better watch your smart-ass mouth before you get choked again."

I knocked on the door, trying to break up the conversation.

The man opened it. "What do you want?"

"I—I—I was looking for Mama," I stuttered.

"Were you listening to us?"

"No, I wasn't."

"Yes, you were."

"No, sir… I wasn't," I said again.

Then he stared a hole through my head and said, "Your mother is busy." And he slammed the door. The man became more openly rude to me after Uncle Joe's coming-out day, even in front of Mama. But Mama only showed me more love.

Often, I'd walk down memory lane and remember it like it was yesterday. Mama didn't mean any harm, but she was always trying to make small talk… the kind that came with correction.

She would say things in the nicest way, like, "Jack, open your legs when you sit, dear. Don't keep them closed together—boys don't sit like that." Or, "Jack, when you talk, try to use your deep voice."

I remember during Christmas, she would say, "Boys don't play with dolls. No, you can't have an Easy-Bake Oven—that's for girls."

When the man started calling me "Boy," I knew that came from that so-called prophet at church—the one telling them to speak things into existence. That foolishness didn't work. I tried. They tried. Everybody tried to help me live up to that penis between my legs… but nothing changed.

Suppose I woke up one day and there it was—a vagina instead of a penis. What would my folks say then? I know Mama would still love me, and the man would probably still hate me. But I would've been one happy chick.

During that time, Mama took me to a priest—but he couldn't help me. She took me to several so-called prophets—they couldn't change me either. She took me to some healing evangelist, and he poured that so-called holy water over my head. That mess was freezing cold.

He tied handkerchiefs around my wrists, ankles, and neck, but that didn't change me. You would've thought he was about to hang me out to dry.

She even took me to a voodoo woman, and ended up losing seven hundred dollars. She asked me not to say a word about it to the man, and I promised I wouldn't. I mean, why should I? I never told her about him taking me to be hypnotized.

I loved Mama, and I knew she wanted the best for me. She didn't want the world looking at me and laughing. I understood that.

But if they had ever asked me what I thought they should do… I would've told them the most logical thing: remove the penis, replace it with a vagina, and let me live my life as the girl I am.

CHAPTER 18

My 18th Birthday; Gone Wrong

The day I turned eighteen was a huge day for me. It was the day I'd been waiting for—the day I was going to make my announcement, telling my family about me… something I've never really been welcomed to do. Sort of like Uncle Joe's coming-out day.

This was a big day for Mama too. She was super excited because I was turning eighteen. She decided to take me shopping, and somehow she persuaded the man to come too. That was… scratchy. Why did the elephant in the room have to come?

Nonetheless, there we were, the three of us. Whenever Mom went to the bathroom or stepped away from our little triangle, he had nothing to say to me. He wouldn't even look my way.

Still, the three of us were out shopping. We quickly got off on the wrong foot. They were trying to get me to like boy stuff, and as you may already know, nothing was appealing to me. Mom was getting frustrated, and the man had nothing to offer but a funky facial expression.

So, me and my smart self decided to pretend to like the bland stuff. After all, let's just get through this part and get out of here. Hey, they can have fun bringing all this stuff back and putting that money right back in their pockets.

I was trying to grow my hair out so I could maybe have long hair for a change. But as a gift from "the man," he wanted to get my hair cut for my birthday. Really? So, off we went to the barber shop. That's all cool, it's just hair; it will grow back. What the heck… I'm almost sure that after my announcement, they're going to allow me to be me. It was nearly killing me, but I put on a really good show.

They bought me a boy's watch, big and ugly. The two of them started having fun, it seemed. But I knew in a few hours all of this was going to change. Their faces would change, their posture would change, and their voices would change too. But my mind was made up. I was going to do it no matter what. Yep, all those changes—but at the end of the day, I would be eighteen, and they would have to go along with my decisions.

When we got home, Mom had me try on the ugly outfits again. I continued to go along with everything, trying to make the moment happy.

Even though I didn't ask to be born, I was still grateful.

Then they surprised me with something I didn't expect. Someone was honking their horn in our yard. Mom yelled from the back room, "Jack, who is that?"

Looking out the window, I answered, "I don't know."

"What type of car is it?" she yelled.

"A black Marquis," I yelled back.

"Is it nice?"

"Yes, I guess—but you might want to come see who it is."

Mom walked in, looked out the window, and said, "Oh, that car. That's a little something your dad and I bought you for your birthday. And that's your sister Jean driving, with that crazy-looking hat on."

I was speechless. Finally, they bought something I really, really liked. I was jumping up and down, like a girl, I suppose. I ran to the car; it was more than I could ever imagine. I was super excited.

And with all that excitement I was showing, I could see the man looking at me like I was disgusting. He saw the girl in full motion, I'm sure of it.

Whatever.

I was eighteen.

I took that baby for a ride. My first car—how exciting! It was perfect. The carpet looked brand new, and the seats did too. I couldn't believe I had a Grand Marquis.

Then I thought about my assignment. I wondered if they would take the car back. I sure hoped not. I doubted they would take something they gave me for my birthday. After all, I'm eighteen now, and I would hope they're going to respect me as an adult.

Mom cooked all my favorite dishes and baked all my favorite sweets. RJ came over, and the two of us snuck off. I told her everything, just like I always do. So she didn't stay as long as she normally would. She did stay long enough to eat, though—because she loves to eat. Come to find out, she was on a diet. She did look smaller, but I figured it was just what she had on.

We had the best time at the table, laughing and enjoying one another. I was still hoping this wasn't going to be our last laugh and dinner together. After dinner, we played a few games and laughed even more.

When everything was done, I said, "Okay, everybody, I have an announcement."

They all thought it was something about college. I had been accepted into several, but I hadn't made up my mind.

RJ literally made her phone ring, pretending it was her grandmother needing her. So, of course, that was her cue to leave—and she did.

We gathered in the living room. Everybody was full. This is how it went.

I stayed standing while everyone else sat down.

I said, "Mom, Dad—I chose Liberty Motion College!"

Everybody shouted. They probably figured I'd choose that one anyway. What they didn't know was I was still liable to change my mind and do something totally different. Because I'm eighteen—I can do that. Nonetheless, they were all happy for me.

My sisters were already attending the college across town. I wanted to go a little further out. They were still depending on our parents for everything. I was hoping that after my first year, I wouldn't have to depend on them for anything.

"Thanks, y'all, but there's one more thing I need to mention." I asked Mom and the man to please, please, please hear me out before they commented. In a playful way, they promised they would keep their lips sealed—acting like they were sealing them and throwing away the key. Even the man was having a little fun.

"Mom, Dad, and family," I said, "I have made another very mature decision. I have decided to be who I am."

My mom blurted out in a laughing tone, "Yes, be who you are, honey," then quickly covered her mouth, stopping herself from laughing out loud. She playfully acted again like she was sealing her lips and throwing away the key for the third time.

"Again," I said with a little laugh, "family, I have decided to be who I am." Taking a deep breath, I let the cat out of the bag.

"Okay, family, here goes." Keep in mind, my sisters already knew I was a girl, but they would have never, in a million years, thought I would just come out and admit it to my folks.

"I, Jack B. Quick, was born with male organs, but with the brain of a female. I understand now that my brain determines who I am—not the meat between my legs. Today, I free myself by accepting who I am. I am a female."

Mom's and the man's eyes lit up, and their expressions changed instantly. I couldn't bear to look at the man's face, so I focused on my mom and my sisters.

"I know you all have worked hard trying to change me into what's between my legs, but the inside of my head is who I really am. I've struggled with this for as long as I can remember. What happened during my development, I can't answer—but the good part is, I know now. I know who I am. And the best part of all… I am finally happy.

Mom, Dad, I love you very much. The clothes you bought me were surely out of love, but that's not what a female would choose to wear. The shoes aren't my cup of tea, but some guy would love them. The watch is for a male, not a female. I'm sorry that I've disappointed you all my life, but whether you accept it or not… this is who I am."

Of course, it was steaming hot in there. But I couldn't stop—I had to make sure all the gaps were covered.

"I'm pretty sure, in the near future, you won't see me coupled with a female. You'll see me with a male, because that's who I'm attracted to. I like everything a girl likes. Okay… that's it.

I'm done. You may unzip your lips—the floor is yours."

The man stood up. "First of all, Jack, you were not born a girl—you were born a boy. You are a boy!"

Before I could even think to stop myself, I spoke. "No, Dad, you don't know that. All you know is that I was born with a penis. How would you know who I am inside unless I tell you? You don't live in my head. I know who I am, just like you know who you are. Did it take your father to tell you who you were? I'm sure it didn't. And neither does it take you to tell me who I am—for I know who I am."

Oh shucks… I'd never talked like this to the man. But I'm eighteen now. I could almost hear Mama saying, "A soft answer turns away wrath, but harsh words stir up anger." That was a scripture she loved from the Bible—and I have to agree with it in some cases.

I realized I may have said way too much and stirred up some anger, but the words just wouldn't stop coming.

So, I toned it down. "I'm sorry. I'm sorry for raising my voice. I'm sorry, Dad. Mom, I'm sorry."

Nonetheless, the damage had been done. Sorry or no sorry.

"Well, Jack," the man said…

But I interrupted again, my big mouth taking over. I felt like this was my last chance to express myself, and I needed to get it all out. I might never have this opportunity again, that's how I felt. And besides, it felt pretty damn good to finally speak my truth.

"Oh, Dad… thanks for making me write those verses over and over again until my fingers were sore, you know, the ones that say people like me should be stoned to death. Those were the very verses that got me thinking. And they finally made me realize that the Bible is fiction. I put it in the same category as Harry Potter and all the other fiction books. If I hadn't done that, I probably would have ended up destroying myself. But thanks to you, I found out there's nothing wrong with me, I'm perfectly fine."

"I see that the number eighteen has caused you to lose your damn mind. I understand that you have chosen to live your life as a faggot, and that's your business."

There my mouth went again…

"I didn't! I didn't choose. And I'm not a faggot. I'm telling you who I am, that's what you fail to hear. I didn't choose! Did you choose? But even if I had chosen, you still should have accepted me."

Oops. I did it again. I talked way too much. And again, I apologized.

"I'm sorry. It's just that you've never given me a chance to talk about me. You've only tried to make me be who you wanted me to be, that's all. I want to be able to talk to you. Not argue… just talk. Can I talk to you about me? About how I feel—just this one time in my life?"

If there were such a thing as the devil's horns, the man had them coming out of his head. He took a step toward me and pointed his finger in my face. Then he said these words:

"If I have to say this again, the undertaker will be scraping your ass off this floor. Do you understand?"

I knew he said what he meant, and he meant what he said.

"Yes, sir… I understand."

He continued where he left off. "So now that you are eighteen and you've chosen hell to be your home, that's your choice. But me and mine will serve the Lord. We'll take the clothes back and get our money back, that's no problem. The car is no longer yours, so give me my damn keys. Your mother is no longer your mother either."

"But… but… how can you speak for Mama?"

"Because I can—that's how."

I looked at Mama, but she wouldn't look at me. I was okay with that, because I knew Mama loved me, whether she said a mumbling word or not. I knew it was all him. He had abused her all these years, just like he'd done me.

The man was livid. I had never heard him use foul language so freely. And he didn't take it back, he didn't even blink. At least I apologized for talking too much. I didn't use foul language, though. Saying I was a girl was foul enough to him.

He wasn't going to make me believe that Mama would erase me from her life. That just wasn't going to happen. I didn't even need to argue that point.

I politely handed him the keys. He snatched them.

"You can count me out as ever being your father. Because you are, and have always been, the devil's child. Get out of my house, now. That's how fast I want you to go. Carry nothing that we've bought you, that includes any clothes or anything else. From now on, I have four children, not five. Do not call me for anything, because I do not know you. As of now, I repeat, I am not your father, so do not refer to me as such. Do I make myself clear?"

I just stood there, looking in his face.

He said it again, but this time he slammed the nearby stand loudly. "Do I make myself clear, dammit!"

"Yes, sir," I said.

He stared at me with that same evil eye, the one he used when he backhanded me, throwing me across the room when I was barely eight or nine years old. The eye that watched me when I walked or sat down. The same eye that burned through me when I fell from the shelf during my ear-hustling days.

Yes… that same eye. The one that caused more damage to my heart than any heart attack ever could. The same eye that haunted me in my sleep when I was a little kid.

When I add it all up, I realize I was abused in the very house where I was supposed to be loved and cared for. I was abused by the person who was supposed to protect me from the bad people.

It got quiet for just a moment, until the man said,

"What do you have to say, Shirley?"

Mama didn't make a sound. She just shook her head.

The man took that head shake as an offense.

"What!" he yelled. "What the hell do you mean you have nothing to say? You have everything in the world to say! This here… thing has stood here and disrespected me when I've done nothing but take care of his—"

Mama ran out, crying.

I dropped my head and cried too. I needed Mama to be there for me, but I understood.

The man shouted again, "Didn't I say get out of my damn house?"

I turned and walked away. My sisters were all wiping tears. I didn't know if it was because they didn't want me to go or because of what I said, I just didn't know.

I had nowhere to go. Nowhere to lay my head. I didn't think the man was going to tell me to get out like that. He knew I had no job and nowhere to go. I started thinking maybe I should have waited, until I had my first apartment and my first job, instead of doing this on my eighteenth birthday.

All I could see in my mind now were the homeless people.

Now I was going to be one.

I never had money to share with them, but I wish I would have at least carried them something from our kitchen.

I looked around my room, and there was nothing, not one thing I could take with me. I didn't need a suitcase. I didn't need a bag. I didn't need anything, because there was nothing to carry.

I came back downstairs, carrying nothing but the tears on my face. Reaching for the door, the man said, "Who bought the clothes on your back?"

I turned around, puzzled.

He said it again. "Who bought the clothes you have on?"

"Y'all did," I said.

"That's what I thought. I said don't carry anything out of this house that I or your mother bought."

So again, I turned around and went back upstairs. I couldn't believe this. What did he expect me to wear?

Then I remembered RJ's clothes she had left under my mattress years ago, just an old dress, way too big for me.

I put the dress on and walked back downstairs barefoot, looking like a crazy person.

The man was still standing in the same spot, with that same mean look on his face.

I reached for the door again, and he said, "Where's the cell phone I bought?"

I looked at him.

"Yes, that too, leave it."

I reached into the pocket of that old dress, took it out, and placed it on the chair in front of me.

I reached for the doorknob once again.

But this time… I walked out.

My sisters had already gone outside, waiting on me, I supposed. They were whispering, telling me they didn't agree with the man and that he was wrong. Jean said she was sorry and that she would never play a trick on me again.

Speaking of that tattoo trick, I guess that was on her mind. But that was years ago. I couldn't figure out why she was still apologizing for it. I told her it was okay. I had forgiven her a long time ago.

Maybe she was just confused.

She reached to hug me, but the man yelled, "Don't touch him, let him go!"

Jean quickly stepped away from me.

I kept walking. The driveway was pretty long, and I knew I looked ridiculous in that huge dress. It was so big it looked like it was floating on its own.

My plan was to call RJ, but I didn't have the phone anymore.

The man was standing in the yard with his arms folded, making sure I left his premises. I guess I wasn't walking fast enough, because he yelled, "Hurry up and get out of my damn yard!"

I felt like he was beating me across my back the whole time.

CHAPTER 19

RJ To The Rescue

Before I could step one foot onto the pavement, RJ pulled up beside me.

"Come on, get in," she said.

I stood there, shaking like a leaf.

RJ got out and wrapped her arms around me, guiding me to the car. I could hear my sisters crying.

Then the man yelled, "Jean! Y'all come inside! He means nothing to me, and he means nothing to y'all. His soul belongs in hell!" RJ heard those stabbing words, but she didn't care. She was there to comfort me no matter what. He couldn't tell her what to do.

Once I got in the car, RJ pulled off swiftly, but only to turn around and come back. She tore up my folks' yard, doing multiple donuts. She had gone mad, no doubt. Grass and dirt flew everywhere, slamming against the house and windows. The flower bed was completely destroyed.

I was yelling, “RJ, no! Don’t! Please stop!”

But that didn’t stop her. She kept spinning in that yard.

When the man stepped out of the house, RJ covered him head to toe with mud and grass. It was devastating.

But she didn’t stop tearing up that yard until she felt satisfied. She wasn’t going to stop, so I stopped begging her.

From there, we went to the car wash. I stayed in the back seat like a dead body, worrying, thinking the cops were going to pull us over any moment.

She finally came to a stop somewhere, but I didn’t bother to lift my head. She didn’t even ask me to get out.

“I’ll be back in a jiff,” she said.

When she returned, she handed me clothes to put on.

“Pull yourself together,” she said. “We have work to do. You will get through this, I promise.”

We pulled up at a bank.

“Why are we stopping here?” I asked.

“You need to open a checking account.”

“A checking account… for what?”

“It’s just a good thing to have,” she replied.

"A good thing to have?" I shouted. "Twenty-five dollars would be a good thing to have too—that's how much it takes to open an account here!"

"I know," she said. "I got it. Come on."

"Oh, you've got twenty-five dollars? Then don't you think it would be wiser to put that in the gas tank?"

"No, come on," she insisted.

I got out like a fool.

"I just got put out, and you want to drag me to a bank just to open a checking account. Why?"

She kept speed-walking like this was some kind of emergency.

Inside, we were immediately asked, "Can I help you?"

RJ pointed at me. "She would like to open an account, sir."

I looked at her like she had lost her ever-loving mind.

But I added, "Yes, I would like to open an account," like I had lost my ever-loving mind too. I didn't want folks thinking we were crazy, so I tried to act intelligent.

It wasn't making sense. I felt like crap, I looked like crap, and I considered myself crap. I didn't care about no bank, no checking account, nothing right then. But the truth was, there I was, literally sitting in a bank trying to open a stupid checking account. I didn't have twenty-five cents, let alone twenty-five dollars.

Finally, the man asked the big question: "How much would you like to open this account with?"

I responded, "How much is required?"—like I had some money.

He said, "The minimum is fifty dollars."

Fifty. I said to myself. Wow. More than I thought. I thought it was twenty-five. My heart sank—I was seconds away from losing it completely.

I said, "Umm..."

RJ jumped in. "She will be depositing ten."

Now, what's wrong with this fool? The man just said the minimum is fifty, and she tells him I'll be depositing ten? How dumb was that! I was so mad, I wanted to scream. I wasn't in the mood for her turning bipolar on me—not today. Dropping my head, I wished I could disappear. That wasn't happening, so I just shut my mouth and let her be the one to make us look like fools.

The man asked, "Are you saying ten dollars because..."

Lord, I really wanted to vanish then.

RJ interrupted him: "Oh, no, sir. Not ten dollars—but ten thousand dollars. She will be depositing ten thousand dollars into her account today."

I raised my sick head. "RJ, please stop; you are killing me." I realized my best friend had literally lost her mind.

Looking at the man, I said, "Please, sir, tell me we're on Candid Camera, because I can't take anymore. I'm so sorry, but this is my best friend, and she's got jokes today. The truth is, I only have twenty-five dollars, so we'll probably be back tomorrow."

I stood to leave.

But RJ pulled out a stack of money and said, "Sir, she has ten thousand dollars, and she will be depositing it into her checking account today."

I stared at her hand, all that money. She whispered, "It's okay, Jackie. The money is good. I haven't robbed a bank or nothing. Remember, I've been waiting on a lump sum from my father's estate for a long time now. So, I finally got it—and I'm giving you ten thousand dollars."

Of course, the man was standing there with his mouth hanging open. I sat there, jaw dropped, in awe.

The man said, "Oh… that is so nice."

I hugged RJ tightly. "Thank you, RJ. I'm so glad you're my best friend. I was literally thinking I was going to have to take care of you because you had lost your mind!"

Tears started rolling down my face again, but this time they were tears of relief.

You never know what life has in store each day. Who would have thought I could walk into a bank with less than a penny and walk out with ten thousand dollars—and I didn't rob or borrow it?

And yep, it was true: RJ had received forty thousand dollars that was due to her.

She had gotten a beautiful two-bedroom apartment. The car she was driving? Totally hers. She even took me to the apartment and said, "This room is yours."

I was blown off my feet. She had decorated it with all my favorite colors and everything I liked—a full room of brand-new, beautiful furniture.

She said, "The rent is nine hundred dollars a month, and we can split it in half."

I said with joy, "Of course!"

Then she added, "But here's the better news: I've already paid the rent for the next twelve months. So don't worry about paying anything until after that."

Wow. It was just too much for one day.

I asked RJ why was she doing so much for me. She smiled and said, "Because you're my best friend. Remember in eighth grade? I told you I was going to protect you."

I remembered her saying that, and I laughed softly. I had wondered back then, how is she even going to protect me?

CHAPTER 20

Mama Did It!

Mama found me, and I was exceptionally glad to see her. She hugged me tightly and said, “Jack, I’m sorry… I am so sorry. Please forgive me.”

“Forgive you for what? You did nothing wrong, Mama.”

“Yes, I did a lot wrong,” she admitted.

“I didn’t stand up for you. You are my child, whether boy or girl, it doesn’t matter. I love you. I’m glad you’re choosing to be who you are, you’re a girl. I’ve known it all your life, but I fought it… partly because of your dad, and mainly because of the Bible.

But never again will I turn my back on you. You explained everything to your dad the day you left. He didn’t understand, or maybe he just refused to, but I understood.

You are right, you would have told us way before now if we had only asked. We made life hard for you when all we had to do was embrace the truth. I see every mistake I made. So I need to know… do you forgive me?"

"Yes, Mama. I forgive you. I know you aren't perfect, and nobody understands everything. Who does? So yes, of course I forgive you. I've thrown it into the sea of forgetfulness."

Hugging me again, she said, "Thank you, dear. I heard RJ call you Jackie—is that the name you prefer?"

"Yes, Ma'am. That is the name I prefer."

"Then, hello, Jackie!"

"Hello, Mama." And we both laughed.

"Jackie… I've gone along with your father way too long. Just like you, I had a plan."

"You did?" I asked, surprised.

"Yes," she said. "That was my plan. I was going to leave your father when you turned eighteen… though I should have left him when you were born."

"What? Why? I mean, I thought you loved him."

"Yes… and no. You saw how he put you out like that, not even shoes on your feet. That wasn't normal. That was cruel. And me, as your mother, allowing it… well, that wasn't normal either.

That was insane of me. I haven't been able to sleep well since the day you left. So, long story short—I'll be moving sooner rather than later."

“What?” I said, excitement rushing through me. “So, you are really leaving Dad?”

“Yes, with bells on.”

“Does he know?”

“Nope, not at all. But he will come home, and I will be gone.”

“Where to?”

“Down below Carterville, in a beautiful five-bedroom house, about an hour and a half from here. I started saving money for a place a few weeks after you were born. The house is nearly paid for, and I already have the keys.”

“What?” I asked, stunned.

She reached into her purse, handed me a card with the address, and gave me my own key. She smiled, “What’s mine is yours. When you get a chance, please go tour our new place. Bring RJ with you, and please tell her thank you for being there for you.

She’s an awesome girl.”

“Do the girls know?” I asked, still in shock.

“No, not at all. I’ve got to keep quiet for now,” she whispered. “Listen, sweetie,” she said softly, “I’ve got to run, I have a doctor’s appointment, but call me using the number on the card.”

She kissed me on the forehead and said, “Jackie, my daughter, hold your head up high. You are an important person in this world. You’ve been through too much not to share your story.”

I sat there for another twenty minutes after Mama left, just thinking. I love that lady. Things were finally looking up for me. Mama accepted me for who I am. For years, I’d longed for this day. I didn’t have to depend on the man for anything anymore. I could live my life and be happy. What more could a girl ask for? I was finally happy.

CHAPTER 21

Mama's Funeral

I was in my room, surfing the web on how to get rid of this penis, when RJ tapped on my bedroom door.

As usual, I said, "Come, come."

"Jackie," she said, "I need to tell you something."

Without looking back, I responded, "Tell me, I'm listening."

"No," she said. "I need your full attention."

Spinning around in my chair, I said, "Okay, I'm listening."

"I'm sorry to tell you this, Jackie, but I just got word that your mom passed."

What? My mom?

"I'm sorry, I am so sorry, Jackie."

"Where did you hear that nonsense? That's not true."

"The girl at the funeral home told me just minutes ago."

"But that can't be true… she was fine. Mama was fine."

"The lady said it was cancer," RJ added softly.

"No… no, that can't be true. Not Mama. I've never heard that she had cancer. It can't be my mama," I whispered, my voice breaking.

RJ's voice was gentle, "The lady at the funeral home said no one knew of her sickness except her—and possibly your dad."

"What lady? Ms. Smith?"

"Yes, her. She said she knew your mom and dad well. One more thing, Jackie, the funeral is today at 1 pm."

I made the dreaded call to the funeral home. It was all true, my mother had died. My sisters hadn't told me, but I later learned the man had threatened them not to. I felt a mix of anger and sadness brewing inside me, anxious to hear the details of that threat.

Squatting beside my bed, I cried until my head throbbed and my eyes were sore. RJ stayed right there, rubbing my back.

Finally, I stood up and glanced at the clock: 12:38. Panic set in. I hurried, hoping I could still make it to the funeral.

Arriving and seeing my family lined up, I jumped out of the car and, almost instinctively, rushed toward my father. I thought, maybe foolishly, that he would hug me, and we'd somehow comfort each other despite everything.

That didn't happen. He just looked at me with that same stupid, angry face he had worn my entire life.

I'm happy to say that face didn't affect me anymore. It didn't mean anything. And he knew it. He knew his power had vanished into thin air. I almost wanted to tell him that, but instead,

I walked away.

I completely forgot about the ass beating I had given him. I suppose he'd never forget it. I could've come back every day for a week and done the same thing, and it still wouldn't have made up for all the years he abused my mom and treated me like crap. He needs to suck it up. He doesn't have the brains to think logically and realize the damage he's caused. Still, that beating carried weight—because it wasn't a stranger who kicked his ass; it was his own child.

My sisters hugged me one at a time, crying. I stood in line beside Jean, my arm around her, trying to hold myself up despite the ton of bricks pressing on my shoulders.

And if things couldn't get worse…

The usher whispered to me, "I'm sorry, but the father of the family said for you to please get out of the line. It's family only."

"But that's my mother in there," I said.

"I'm so sorry, I didn't know. He must have meant someone else," she said and walked off.

A minute later, the same woman returned. "The father of the family said, please get out of the family line. If you would… this isn't a time to fight, so please do as he wishes."

I slowly loosened my hold on Jean's shoulder and walked to the very back.

I walked in with the crowd—friends and strangers alike. I took an obituary from the usher and kept moving with everyone else. I almost passed by Uncle Joe, but he stood and gave me the hug my dad should have given me.

I walked up to see Mama for the last time… and I broke down right there. I wanted to be dead instead of her. Not too long ago, I had those same thoughts, and now they were warring inside me again.

With the help of the usher, I pulled myself together and took my seat.

As I read the obituary, tears streamed down my face, until I realized it was about to get worse. It said my mother was survived by her husband and four daughters. It didn't mention me. It didn't mention Uncle Joe either. I don't know about him, but that hurt.

I've been hurt so much by this man, you'd think I wouldn't feel it anymore.

Then he gave the tribute. He spoke about the good times the family had with Mama, naming every child one by one, except me.

I didn't exist.

All of a sudden, something shifted inside me. The pain didn't go away, but it changed. It turned into something else… something stronger. Like the feeling I had when I stood up for RJ before. It wasn't anger this time, it was boldness. I didn't want to fight. I just wanted to speak. I wanted to be heard.

It felt strange, but it felt good.

So when Mrs. Barrett said, "At this time, we will have remarks," and started calling the names listed in the program, of course, mine wasn't one of them, I got up anyway.

I walked to the front and took the microphone.

Who was going to stop me?

Nobody.

"Good evening. My name is Jack Quick. This lovely and beloved lady lying before us today is my mother, my biological mother. She loved me unconditionally, even when she didn't understand me."

Out of the corner of my eye, I saw my dad shifting in his seat, unable to get comfortable. He didn't expect me to come forward, and he had no idea what I was about to say.

Then I said, "Due to my father's wishes, my name was not written in the obituary, nor was I allowed to walk in with my family today."

I could see people straighten up, their ears perked like they were ready to hear what was coming next.

"You see, on my eighteenth birthday, I confessed some things to my father. Because of that confession, I was immediately dismissed from my daddy's house. While living there, I tried to change who I was into who my dad wanted me to be. But you see, I came into this world with something much deeper than what the eyes can see. Somewhere along the way, while growing in my mother's womb, I developed the body of a male, so society labeled me a boy. But my dad refused to accept that I was also born with the mind of a female. Confusing, right? Of course. Nevertheless, it caused a war between my father and me my entire life.

Yes, I'm what my dad calls a trifling something, set to burn in hell. Trifling… meaning someone unimportant, someone not worthy to be loved. And that's how he made me feel all my life. But I'm not trifling. Not at all."

Turning to my dad, I said, "Dad, I can't say I'm sorry for who I am. But I will say I'm sorry for every pain and every uncomfortable moment I've caused you, including the discomfort you feel right now.

With all I've been through, you'd think I would give up, right, Dad? But I can't. There are too many people like me who need to hear my story. I will hold my head up—and I will hold it high—because I am somebody. And I am somebody important. That's what my mom told me, and I'm sticking to it."

"There are two other people I must recognize today. One is my mother's brother—Uncle Joe. Uncle Joe, would you please stand?"

"This man is my mother's only brother. He has been one of her greatest sources of strength. More than any man on this earth, he stood by her through thick and thin. Yet his name wasn't placed in the obituary either. But that's okay—because he knows who he is."

"The other person is my best friend, RJ… she's not here today."

"I'm here, friend!" RJ yelled from the back.

"Wow," I said, dropping my head with a small giggle.

"That's exactly what I mean. That girl became my first real friend in middle school. She listened to me, and never once did she put me down—instead, she supported me one hundred percent. I don't know where I would have ended up if it hadn't been for her.

And if my mom had known all the things this girl helped me through, she would have claimed her as her daughter too."

"But you, Dad… I don't know your story. I don't know what you went through. But it must have been something awful for you to turn out so cruel, so mean, so lowdown. And I hope you know by now, your bullying power is gone. It's gone, Dad. It's gone.

And I know you told me not to call you Dad or even acknowledge you as such—but here's the thing: when I remove you from my mouth and from my mind, it will be when I decide to, not you. Your angry face doesn't move me anymore, and your words don't control me.

But I still love you… and I wish the best for you."

Placing the microphone back in the hands of the person in charge, I walked to my seat with my head held high—just like Mama told me.

Jean stood first and started a slow, steady clap. My other sisters followed. Then the whole congregation—including Uncle Joe, rose to their feet, clapping as if the president had just spoken.

Everyone was standing.

Everyone… except the man.

As I walked back to my seat, I thought to myself, wow… I'm actually an adult now. The only place I'd ever given a speech before was in my bathroom mirror.

While everyone was still clapping, my dad walked out.

If I ever wrote a book about him, it would be titled: ***"The Stone Man."***

CHAPTER 22

Save The Day

That evening, after the funeral, Jean called me—but somehow, I missed it. The message went like this:

"We are at the Sweet Creams Apartment complex, trying to get an apartment. Dad put us out. He gave us orders before the funeral not to talk to you if you showed up. According to him, we deliberately disobeyed him, like Adam disobeyed God. We were given fifteen minutes to be gone."

Jean managed to sneak out Mama's pictures, jewelry, and purse. When she mentioned the purse, I had a flashback of my conversation with Mama. Crazy—I hadn't thought about it even once until that moment.

I took off to Sweet Creams Apartments.

The four of them were sitting at a table with red eyes. Jean was wiping tears when I walked in. I was actually excited—

because I was about to bring in the sunshine. I love bringing in the sunshine.

When I walked in, they all looked at me, greeting me with quiet nods. But the lady at the desk took a second look and said,

"Wow, I didn't know it was five of y'all. Are you the oldest girl or the youngest?"

Jean quickly answered,

"She's our youngest sister."

"Yes," I added,

"I'm the youngest girl—and I've come to save the day."

"Save the day?" the lady asked.

"Yes, save the day."

I walked over to the table and gently took the pen out of each of their hands—they were about to sign their little John Hancocks. As I took each pen, I repeated,

"You won't need this… you won't need this… you won't need this… and you won't need this."

Jean looked at me, frustrated.

"Jack, we don't have time for games right now. What are you doing?"

"I'm giving you something in place of those pens," I said, "because you won't be needing a pen today."

I reached into my pocket and handed each of them a key, starting with Jean.

"This is yours."

"This is yours."

"This is yours."

"And this is yours."

They looked just like I did when I thought RJ had lost her mind at the bank.

"You didn't know it," I said,

"but Mama bought a house before she died. The house is ours—paid in full. And here's the address."

I handed them the card. The four of them stared at it like it wasn't real. Then they broke down, crying in that office like babies.

Thank God Jean still had that old car Uncle Joe gave her for winning that cooking contest. Jean later told me they had loaded up in that car with nothing but the clothes on their backs—because Dad said,

"Don't carry nothing else out of here."

But before pulling off, Jean had a thought. She called the police. When the officer arrived, he ordered Dad to let them go back in and get all their belongings, right then and there. Boy, was he furious. But that little car got loaded up real quick.

My sisters swore they would never have anything to do with him again, even if he was dying.

But not me.

One of the many things Uncle Joe taught me was to "charge it to his ignorance, not his heart."

That wasn't easy to do… but I tried.

CHAPTER 23

Sharing My Kidney; Gone Wrong

We found out that Dad was sick and in need of a kidney. I spoke with my sisters about the five of us—maybe one of our kidneys could work for him. They said no without hesitation and refused to discuss it any further. But me? I tossed and turned all night thinking about it.

The next morning, there were no ifs, ands, or buts about it.

I was going to at least try to help. I made one call, and the ball started rolling. I headed to the hospital, ignoring the fact that the man hadn't reached out to me in over two years. Though I had whipped his ass good, it couldn't even compare to the damage he had done to me as a kid.

To make a long story short, I did it—my kidney was a perfect match. I was ecstatic. I felt good knowing the man would be well again. The nurses knew that Mr. Quick was my father, and they also knew I didn't want him to know I was the donor.

A couple of days later, I received a call—my dad was asking if it was possible to meet the "Good Samaritan." He wanted to thank them personally. Because of the excitement, I agreed.

I arrived at Trent Best Hospital around 2 p.m. on a beautiful Thursday afternoon. The nurses were kind and seemed genuinely excited to break the news.

It appeared the nurses liked Dad. That was strange because most people didn't. To me, it was a sign that the man had changed for the better.

I was asked to stand outside the door while they went in to break the news that I was there. From that point, they would signal for me to enter. That was the plan.

"Mr. Quick," one of the nurses said, "are you ready to meet the Good Samaritan who donated this wonderful kidney to you?"

Dad's voice came strong: "Yes, ma'am, I am."

"Okay, awesome! Come on in, Mr. Good Samaritan," she politely called to me.

Taking a deep breath and stretching just a little, I walked in with a smile on my face. The man took one look at me and dropped his head into the palm of his hand as if he were crying.

The nurses and I waited silently, but Dad just sat there, face buried in his hands.

One of the nurses whispered, "Oh, that's so sweet. He's overwhelmed with joy. Let's give him a moment alone," and suggested we step out.

We all left, and I headed down to the dining room, feeling happy because I'd made my father the happiest man in the world. I was grateful that I could be there for him at such a pivotal moment in his life.

Sitting with my coffee, I wondered what was going through Dad's mind. Was he thinking about apologizing for the past? Did he have so much to say that he didn't know how to start? Maybe he was remembering my mother's funeral and how cold he had been to me. Perhaps he was stunned that, after everything, I had come to his rescue.

One thing I knew for sure: I had totally forgiven him. I had thrown all the pain, anger, and resentment into the sea of forgetfulness. We all make mistakes sometimes. And just because someone is an adult doesn't mean they're exempt from learning, growing, or being forgiven.

After thirty minutes of daydreaming, I returned to my father's room. Taking a deep breath, I opened the door—and froze. Before I could take a single step inside, I saw my father hanging from the ceiling, a chair tipped beneath him.

I screamed for help. Nurses came running from all directions.

I stood back, hands over my mouth, completely frozen. Confusion swirled through me like a storm. And then my eyes caught the whiteboard. My father had written his supposed last words: "I would rather be dead."

I didn't know what to do, so I ran.

I ran through the hospital, tears flying backward, pounding down the stairs to the ground floor. I ran past my car and down the sidewalk, with no destination in mind. I had no idea how long I had been running before I tripped and fell into a flower garden. I didn't even try to get up; I just lay there, overwhelmed.

A hand rested on my shoulder. RJ. I had no idea how she had found me.

"Jackie, it's going to be alright, I promise," she said softly.

She took me home and nursed me back to life with her usual words of encouragement. I didn't know if the nurses had saved Mr. Quick or not. I didn't lift a finger to find out. It didn't matter anymore. For real this time, I knew it was over. He was as good as dead—but I still didn't hate him.

Not long after that kidney disaster, I had a dream. It was wild at first, chaotic, but somehow it made perfect sense. In the dream, I had officially changed my name to Jackie Elizabeth Owens.

Shortly after, I did it for real. My name was legally changed from Jack B. Quick to Jackie Elizabeth Owens. Owens was my mom's maiden name, and Elizabeth my grandmother's first name.

My sisters followed suit, each legally changing their last names from Quick to Owens. They thought it was the coolest dream ever. I felt incredible after the change, as if I had severed the bloodline that tied me to that man.

And yes, I did get my kidney back. I told the staff not to volunteer any information about Mr. Quick. I didn't want to hear it.

Finally, I was free. Finally, I was Jackie.

CHAPTER 24

Rj's Excitement

RJ called me while I was at the library—loud and frantic. She insisted I step outside immediately because what she had to say was urgent.

"Oh, it better be good," I said, half-joking.

You would have thought she won the Mega Millions. But no—it was a story about a flat tire. On some back road, coming home from a meeting.

She was freaking out because she didn't know how to change a tire. Then her phone died, and she couldn't find her charger. There she was, stranded on a back road with no phone and a flat.

RJ is almost as small as me now. She's lost 102 pounds since she last checked, and her confidence is through the roof. She looks amazing. But back to the flat tire.

Suddenly, someone pulled up behind her. She didn't know whether to panic or hope for help. To her surprise, the person walking to her window was Jackson. Yes, Jackson—the guy she had been secretly crushing on all through school.

Back then, RJ never spoke two words to him, and he never spoke two words to her. But she'd been in love.

Jackson had gone to school for automotive and was now a professional mechanic. He had his toolbox with him and knew exactly what to do. RJ said they ended up laughing and having fun while he worked.

When he was finished, she asked,

"How much do I owe you?"

He grinned.

"It's pretty high."

"Really?" she asked.

"Yep. A ten-digit number," he replied.

"A ten-digit number?" she questioned, confused.

"Yes," he said with a smirk. "Your cell phone number is my fee."

She shared her number, and they drove off happy as could be. RJ said she was so excited that she barely remembered the drive home—just walking in the front door in a daze.

She's such a sweet girl; she deserves the best.

I gave her the same advice my Uncle Joe once gave me: Don't be too anxious. Don't carry the conversation; let him do that. Keep it slow. If it's meant to be, it will be. Never run after a man; let him chase you. A man is a hunter by nature.

RJ laughed.

"Don't worry," she said. "After ignoring me in high school, he deserved to sweat a little."

Well, it's been four years since we graduated high school. I sat there thinking about all the changes I've made since then.

Let's see… I finally let my hair grow down my back, just like I've always wanted. I dress like a girl all the time now, and I feel good about myself—better than I've ever felt in my entire life. The amazing thing is that when people recognize me at all, they always connect me to being one of the quadruplets. That's pretty cool.

Most people wouldn't guess that I have a penis between my legs, but sadly, I do. I haven't dated anyone yet, but that's okay. I've got my whole life ahead of me.

Not a day goes by that I don't think about my mama. I knew her so well; sometimes it feels like she's still right here with me. And I like that.

CHAPTER 25

Surprise!

Three times a month, I volunteered at the dialysis center. I love caring for people. I think I had a nervous breakdown after giving my kidney, well, I don't know much about nervous breakdowns, but it seems to fit the description. Still, I'm happy again, and that's exactly how Mama would want me to be.

I was doing my usual rounds, checking on patients during their treatment, walking around the room with my usual jolly, friendly energy. Everyone loved me, and the feeling was mutual.

Then I noticed someone sitting with his head down, looking uncomfortable. I gently tapped him on the shoulder.

"Are you okay?"

"I'm doing well, ma'am," he replied, lifting his head.

And there he was. The man. My eyes may have lingered a second too long, but I played it off perfectly. Before realizing who I was, he had called me "ma'am." You and I both know he would never have said that if he'd seen me first.

I smiled and said,

"Good, sir. Glad to hear that,"

and moved on. I could feel his stare the whole time, and that was fine with me. He was welcome to look.

I hadn't seen him in three years. I didn't know if he was alive or dead, but there he was in living color, and I was happy. I had told him the day he threw me out that I was going to live my life as a female, and I meant it.

He was propped up with a cane, for whatever reason. I wish him no harm, but I've moved on. I surround myself only with positive people. I know I shocked him, my hair was long, flowing down my back, draped elegantly over one shoulder with a pretty braid finished with a cute little ribbon. I'm sure he wondered about… well, you know.

I had on a soft blue straight-line skirt just above my knees, a pink shirt, and a neatly plaited vest that made the outfit pop. I had already received four compliments that morning, and I wasn't ashamed, not after he saw me. If anything, I felt pretty damn good. At least he knows I didn't crumble, that I didn't die.

It feels amazing to be a grown-up, able to make my own decisions. One day, I hope to adopt and be an incredible mother, just like my mama. And thanks to the school of hard knocks I got from him, I already know exactly how not to parent. I'll be the opposite of him, and I'll be awesome.

CHAPTER 26

At The Rink

RJ and I were at the skating rink, our usual Saturday night spot. But tonight was special—it was the night of the big skate dance, and I was part of it. The rink was packed, buzzing with energy, lights flashing across the polished floor. Honestly, I'm a pretty good skater, if I do say so myself, but nothing could have prepared me for what happened next.

I saw him: the dream of my life, Robert L. Northerner, my high school crush. My knees went weak; my stomach did somersaults. I was shaking in my boots, no lie. I bolted straight for the bathroom, out of breath, heart pounding. RJ came running after me, laughing, hands over her mouth. She knew exactly how crazy I had been about Robert, even though he never spoke a word to me in school. I don't even think he noticed me back then.

We stumbled out of the restroom, and I collapsed onto the nearest bench, trying to collect myself. Robert wasn't alone—he had two kids with him, maybe twins, eight or nine years old. I assumed they were his little brothers or cousins.

But the moment we tried to find him again, he had vanished. We searched everywhere, but he and the kids were gone. I sighed, brushing it off.

"Guess he's gone," I told RJ. "But it was a pleasure seeing him again."

I laced up my skates and glided onto the rink. RJ was already there, her energy infectious. The music started, a signal for everyone to grab the waist of the person in front of them. We formed a huge circle, and the dance began.

The big overhead light was turned off, leaving the designer lights on the floor to create a kaleidoscope of color. When the music hit a certain beat, we grabbed hands, spinning into multiple circles, weaving in and out of each other with dizzying precision. The energy was electric, the movements flawless, pure joy. You almost had to be there to grasp the beauty of it all.

So there I was, reaching out and taking the hand of the person to my left, skating around the rink with all the other couples. You really had to come to practice to know the steps, but I felt confident. I glanced down at my partner—and lo and behold, it was Robert Northerner. My heart jumped. I was supposed to faint, but the old fear was gone. This time, I knew I wasn't dreaming. He was smiling, and I couldn't help but smile back.

The night was phenomenal. I was holding hands with the guy of my dreams—for real! From that moment, we danced without letting go. Even when the slow song came on, our hands never parted.

He leaned closer and asked my name, and for the rest of the night, we couldn't take our eyes off each other. I felt that old flutter of nerves, but it wasn't fear—it was excitement, pure and dizzying.

But as the night wound down, reality crept back in. I didn't want Robert to know about me—about my penis. So when he walked away to help the little kids, I grabbed RJ's hand, and we hurried out like Cinderella escaping before midnight.

RJ thought I was crazy at first, but I didn't care. I had just experienced something magical—something I might never experience again—and I wasn't about to ruin it with my life story. I thought about my eighth-grade dance, all the awkwardness, and realized this time was different. I was dancing with the right person, and there was no man around to embarrass me.

RJ and I stayed up half the night, laughing until our stomachs hurt, racing each other to the bathroom, and telling ridiculous stories. That girl is hilarious, even if she doesn't realize it herself. She keeps me laughing like nobody else ever could.

CHAPTER 27

The Last Thing To Go

After my encounter with Robert Northerner, I couldn't stop thinking about this penis. I wanted it gone. No more hiding. No more half-lives of pretending. It was time to take action.

I scheduled a visit with my doctor, and we got the ball rolling. The journey to becoming fully myself had officially begun. RJ was over the moon for me—she's the only person who knows my story inside and out, and her excitement made everything feel even more real.

Before surgery, I completed several therapy sessions. My doctor strongly recommends them for all his patients, and I could see why. It wasn't just preparation for the surgery—it was preparation for my new life. Soon, I would have a real vagina, and the thought made my heart race with anticipation.

Sleep became impossible. I barely ate, only enough to keep my body functioning, because I was too excited. I wished my mother were here. She would have been so proud, so happy. I could almost hear her whispering encouragement, smiling at the steps I was finally taking to claim the life I deserved.

And then it happened. The surgery. The transformation. The moment I had dreamed about my whole life. When I woke up, I felt a surge of joy I'd never experienced before, the penis was gone. My body finally matched my mind. My heart soared. I had a vagina.

It was the happiest day ever. Everything went perfectly. Every ounce of fear, every sleepless night, every tear, it had all been worth it. I was finally, completely, me.

CHAPTER 28

Meeting Uncle Reddy!

This particular morning, I woke up to a beautiful, sunny, yet windy day. And it just happened to be Valentine's Day. I had so much to be grateful for. My surgery alone was reason enough to celebrate, and to top it off, my recovery had been a breeze—far easier than I ever imagined.

My plan for the day was simple but perfect. First, I wanted to head to the mall and buy myself something pretty. Then, after picking up my little indulgence, I planned to catch a movie and enjoy a giant bag of buttered popcorn—Greatlakes Cinema was famous for it. After that, a little horseback riding at my friend's farm would round out the day. A perfect day, or so I thought…

I had just stepped out of the shower when I heard the doorbell. Naturally, I assumed it was the postman. I couldn't let him get away; he wouldn't leave my package unless I signed for it.

I dried off quickly, slipped into my panties, threw on my robe, and ran for the door—but I was too late.

Instead of a package, I found a note. It simply read: "Uncle Reddy."

That was it. No explanation. No preamble. Just Uncle Reddy. My heart skipped a beat. Uncle Reddy… at my door? Really? Could this be true?

I peeked through the window and caught sight of him! That head—so distinct, so unmistakably his. But just as quickly, he had pulled back into traffic and was moving down the street, fading from view. My mind raced. What on earth was he doing here? And why now?

All I could do was hope the traffic and the traffic lights would stall him. I was ready to run like my life depended on it. My only hope was to catch him at that last traffic light before he disappeared completely.

Tucking the note into my robe pocket, I bolted. Corners were cut, flower beds were jumped, and my long legs ate up the pavement like they had a mind of their own.

A barking dog joined the chase. I didn't even glance back to see what kind of dog it was. What that dog didn't realize? There wasn't a single dog in town that could catch me.

I fell twice along the way, but each time, I sprang up without missing a beat. Finally, I made it across the street—but there was still more ground to cover.

I'm sure my robe was flying behind me, giving the world a glimpse of my pink panties. But honestly, that was the least of my concerns. Catching Uncle Reddy was everything. The uncle who left home as a teen under mysterious circumstances, the one who sent gifts every Christmas yet remained a stranger, the only uncle

I'd ever wanted to meet. This was my shot, and I was not letting it slip.

The wind was fierce, threatening to take my robe entirely. I could have run faster if I'd ditched it, but then the cops would've had a reason to chase me too.

No matter what, I had to reach him. I didn't know how he'd found me, but he did, and that was all that mattered.

I made it! There he was, sitting at the last traffic light, casually sipping a bottle of water. The worst-case scenarios were running through my head: what if I had the wrong guy? Or what if the light turned green and he ran me over?

I had to literally dart into the street, rush around the front of his car, and tap on his window. I told myself: if I make a fool out of myself, it won't be the first time, and it surely won't be the last. So, whatever happens, happens.

"Jackie!" I yelled, holding up the piece of paper with his name on it.

He immediately broke into a huge smile. "Hop in, Jack!"

He knew my name! Well, of course he knew my name, it's just not Jack anymore—but still. I was way too excited to care.

We spent a good minute just laughing before we could even think about talking. Uncle Reddy had a unique, pleasant laugh—the kind that makes you start laughing even if nothing's funny. And that's exactly what happened. We laughed our butts off right there in the street.

Then I spotted the postman, headed straight for me. My laughter vanished instantly. "I'm sorry, Uncle Reddy, but I've got to run again. I need to catch that postman. Please turn around and come back to my apartment—I'll meet you there."

He burst out laughing. "You've got to be kidding."

"Nope, not kidding," I said, starting to move again. "I have to sign for the package he's bringing me. If I'm not there, he'll take it back."

"But if you give me a minute," Uncle Reddy offered, still laughing, "I can just turn around and take you back."

"I'm sorry, Uncle Reddy, I don't have a minute to spare. Plus, it's going to take you more than a minute to turn around in all this traffic. I'll see you at the house!"

And with that, I bolted—the same way I'd come. Behind me, I could hear Uncle Reddy laughing like he couldn't believe I was running again.

But yeah, the moment Uncle Reddy opened his mouth, I knew he was gay… and that's cool. I'm just saying—the truth's in the pudding. I was right about the skeleton in the closet. I'm still proud of him. Hey, a girl loves a good story, and I couldn't wait to hear his.

I jumped the same flower bed and ran from the same dog. This time my foot got stuck in a hole, and I had to struggle a second to get it out. After that, I was hopping and running at the same time. I didn't know if I'd bruised my foot or not, but I didn't have time to find out. I had to catch that postman!

When it was all said and done, my ankle was just fine. I must admit, this day will be written down in my history book. And I would do it all over again—just to catch the postman and my Uncle Reddy; both of them were worth every second.

Finally, I got to the apartment. Uncle Reddy was waiting with a huge grin. He opened his arms wide and gave me a hug that made me feel like we'd known each other forever. "This is a very special day for me, Jack," he said. "A very special day. You are my niece, and it's quite the pleasure to meet you."

His voice had a familiar warmth, it reminded me a little of the man, especially when I caught the side profile.

We laughed and talked for hours. Uncle Reddy filled in a lot of missing pieces about the man. He told me their parents had always had negative things to say about gay people, and often claimed the God of the Bible hated them.

He laughed softly. "Mom got offended when I asked her if God made gay people. She said, 'Yes and no. He made them, but he didn't make them gay; they did that themselves.'"

I almost choked on my words. "How stupid was that?" he continued. "My brothers and I decided a long time ago that we wanted no part of their religion. We would have a miserable life trying to live up to it."

I asked cautiously, "Oh… you and one of your other brothers were both gay?"

"Oh, I'm sorry for going ahead of myself," he said. "My parents had twins three times. So, the total number of children was six. Yes, my mom gave birth to six boys. Your dad was the only straight one."

"What! Five gay brothers?" I exclaimed, my mouth hanging open in disbelief. Uncle Reddy chuckled. "You can close your mouth now," he said. We laughed even harder, but he continued.

"We gained strength from one another," he said. "Though my brothers and I were all gay, we were still different; two of us enjoyed dressing like females, the rest of us didn't. I preferred dressing like a male. We got along well and supported each other.

Your dad knew we were gay since we were kids. He had little to nothing to say to us even then. He thought we were strange and stupid—the feeling was mutual.

"At school, he told people we weren't brothers. Which was fine; it didn't bother us in the least. We had each other, and we didn't need his negative energy.

"Our mother and father separated when we were in our early teens. It was crazy because we found out later that our dad was gay too. That was… weird. Because he, too, would bad-mouth gay people constantly." I still haven't figured that part out.

"So, Uncle Reddy," I asked, "was that the reason you left home early?"

"Yes, absolutely. And also, I had met someone I cared for deeply. Yep, I sure did."

"How was life in school?" I asked. "Was it hard?"

I was asking plenty of questions, still trying to digest the fact of five gay brothers. Uncle Joe didn't even know that—at least he hadn't mentioned it to me. And I was sure having five gay brothers had added a lot of weight to the man's mental state.

"School?" Uncle Reddy said, shaking his head. "Not really.

Because when one of us was bullied at school, that bully had to take on all five of us. And we all could fight. We weren't scared of anyone. Plus, Mama put us all in some type of self-defense class at a very young age. That class gave us confidence. She knew we were going to have to protect ourselves from the bullies."

"When your dad went to jail, we heard he was bullied by a gay guy. We would have jumped that guy, but we didn't know the full story. From that day to this one, we never found out if anything actually went down. Personally, I don't think so," Uncle Reddy said.

"Wow," I laughed. "I remember Mom asking Dad if he had any gays in his family. And he said, not that he knew of."

Uncle Reddy threw his head back and laughed so hard it echoed through the room. He cut it off quickly and said, "He lied." We laughed even more.

"Our parents were very religious too. So, that of course made life harder for the seven of us. We were taught that God was going to burn even the children in hell, especially if they were gay. So, you know how that went. My brothers and I didn't believe that stuff.

"Even so, how could you be friends with someone—or something—that threatened to burn your children forever? How loving is that? And anytime someone threatens to harm you if you don't do what they want, that's bullying.

"If I was invited to a birthday party and didn't want to go, why would the birthday person be in the right to burn me at all?

That's how foolish it is. I mean, stuff like that happens in real life, but it's called bullying. Well, my brothers and I disapproved of bullies.

"So, my folks' holy book was inviting everyone to heaven, but we didn't want to go… Now what? Yeah, your inviter must burn us… forever!"

I truly enjoyed hearing Uncle Reddy's stories about his upbringing. We vowed to keep in touch from now on. He was excited to meet the other girls, and I was excited to meet all my uncles.

It had gotten late in the evening when Uncle Reddy finally left. I only had time to take another shower and head to the mall before it got too late. All my plans for today were pretty much washed down the drain—but that was okay because I had already had a perfect and wonderful day, none of which had been planned.

I spruced myself up and headed for the door, feeling good and looking cute. Before I could open it, the doorbell rang. I knew it had to be Uncle Reddy coming back for something he forgot. But when I opened the door, I froze. There stood Robert L. Northerner, holding a box of candy and a dozen roses.

www.ingramcontent.com/pod-product-compliance
Lightning Source LLC
LaVergne TN
LVHW050647100826
845148LV00011B/2020

* 9 7 9 8 2 3 4 0 5 7 6 6 2 *